PETTY LIES

PETTY LIES

A Novel

SULMI BAK

TRANSLATED BY SARAH LYO

MULHOLLAND BOOKS
LITTLE, BROWN AND COMPANY
NEW YORK BOSTON LONDON

The characters and events in this book are fictitious. Any similarity to real persons, living or dead, is coincidental and not intended by the author.

Copyright © 2025 by Sulmi Bak

Hachette Book Group supports the right to free expression and the value of copyright. The purpose of copyright is to encourage writers and artists to produce the creative works that enrich our culture.

The scanning, uploading, and distribution of this book without permission is a theft of the author's intellectual property. If you would like permission to use material from the book (other than for review purposes), please contact permissions@hbgusa.com. Thank you for your support of the author's rights.

Mulholland Books / Little, Brown and Company
Hachette Book Group
1290 Avenue of the Americas, New York, NY 10104

mulhollandbooks.com

First Edition: November 2025

Mulholland Books is an imprint of Little, Brown and Company, a division of Hachette Book Group, Inc. The Mulholland Books name and logo are trademarks of Hachette Book Group, Inc.

The publisher is not responsible for websites (or their content) that are not owned by the publisher.

The Hachette Speakers Bureau provides a wide range of authors for speaking events. To find out more, go to hachettespeakersbureau.com or email hachettespeakers@hbgusa.com.

Little, Brown and Company books may be purchased in bulk for business, educational, or promotional use. For information, please contact your local bookseller or the Hachette Book Group Special Markets Department at special.markets@hbgusa.com.

Print book interior design by Taylor Navis

ISBN 978-0-316-59448-6 (HC); 978-0316-59450-9 (e-book)

LCCN is available at the Library of Congress

Printing 1, 2025

LSC-C

Printed in the United States of America

ALSO BY SULMI BAK

The Silence of the Swan
Dalwhinnie Hotel

PETTY LIES

1.
I AM A BAD TUTOR
[MIRA'S LETTER]

Hello, Yujae's mother.

I expect you're wondering why I've suddenly written you a letter. Before I give my reasons, I'd like you to know that four-fifths of this letter had already been written by the time I started tutoring your son.

You may need to pay attention from now on as you read my letter, as I'm about to discuss events that happened one year ago.

Yes, I know.

Why now bring up the far-distant past? you're thinking. But since those events matter more to me than anything else, so much so that I remember them as clearly as if they happened yesterday, I hope you'll read this letter to the end.

Do you remember the incident last year, when the mutilated body of a dog, a black dachshund, was discovered in front of the public restroom in the park?

From now on, I'll call the dog "Bell."

A year ago, a barely five-year-old Bell slipped out through the front door, which his owner had propped open to let in some fresh air, and was wandering about in the streets. I assume you know about the territorial nature of dogs. Unlike cats, who attempt to defend their domain, dogs have a strong instinct to widen theirs. It's for this reason that they urinate on roadside trees and utility poles. And more so than any other animal, dogs have an irrepressible curiosity. Surely, it's only natural that an animal like that would want to know what the world outside looked like and whether they might find new friends.

After leaving the house, Bell scampered off without a backward glance. In his excitement, he'd even have forgotten to mark his territory against every utility pole in sight. Much later, a thought would have struck him: My mother will be looking for me—have I traveled too far from home? And then the dog would have grown more and more frightened.

What's your take on this, Ms. Moon? Suppose your child has lost his way. Imagine that your child, scarcely five years of age, is wandering about in the streets. In the space of an instant, wouldn't his curiosity about that unfamiliar world transform into fear? It might happen to anyone, not just children. Left stranded in a strange place, adults are just as likely to go mad with terror—and in some extreme cases, even to the point of harming themselves.

And yet, perhaps because dogs are such loyal creatures, Bell would have known his owner would be upset if anything awful were to happen to him, and he'd have tried to find a way back home by any means possible.

But that night, Bell was discovered as a corpse. His cervical vertebrae had been completely shattered.

Did you know that the bones of the neck are not easily broken?

Attached directly to the rest of the spine, the cervical vertebrae are closely linked to one's rate of survival, which means they're one of the most intricate and vital parts of the body. That's why they don't easily fracture, as a rule. But the same bones will also splinter like wooden chopsticks if someone twisted them with all the force in their arms. Even if you were lucky enough to survive such an attack, you'd end up becoming disabled.

Did Bell not have even that little bit of luck?

Since the cervical vertebrae won't fracture unless brute force is applied, fractured cervical vertebrae can mean only one thing. That's murder. Without one last embrace from his owner, the poor dog had been murdered near his home.

How on earth had things come to this point?

Whose fault was it? Bell's for having run outside, unable

to suppress his instincts? Or was it his owner's for failing to be more attentive? You might say both were at fault.

But everyone's bound to make a mistake. Every living creature makes mistakes. Even monkeys sometimes fall out of trees.

The worst kind of act isn't done out of ignorance; it's an act that is committed knowingly.

You should never turn a blind eye to a willful act. Yet what are things like in reality? The courts permit sexual offenders with recidivism rates of up to 100 percent to reenter society; schools keep quiet to cover up bullying incidents; and cases of animal cruelty are ruled simple negligence. That's because society is always on the side of the powerful. It is society that favors adults over children, men over women, the wealthy over the poor, humans over animals, and the able-bodied over disabled persons.

Do you know about the Somang incident, by any chance?

On the eighteenth of August in 2011, two assailants stoned a suspected three-year-old dog on a construction site in the middle of the public square of Gwanghwamun. For forty minutes they threw rocks at the dog, which they'd cornered beside a container, because they thought it was barking too loudly. For that reason alone, they'd tried to kill a dog unable to put up a fight. The dog managed to cling to life but suffered a ruptured right eye, damage to the brain, and fractures in her front legs and paws. Her condition was so critical that no one would have thought it strange if she'd died on the spot. It was a miracle that Somang was still alive, people said. But how did the court sentence the two assailants? All they received were light fines of one million won and five hundred thousand won, respectively.

Was it because they only had the intent to kill and didn't go so far as to kill?

Or was the dog undervalued because it was a stray?

Then how would you explain the Eunbi incident in June 2010, which resulted in a mere two-hundred-thousand-won fine? The cat—who was brutally murdered by a female neighbor—plainly had an owner. It had been wandering around, having simply lost its way, like Bell. Instead of returning the cat to its owner, however, the attacker tortured it in confinement with ruthless and unrelenting violence before tossing it off a high-rise building. When the incident became widely known, the assailant—rather than reflect on her crimes—went after the cat's owner to assault and threaten him.

How about the following cases?

In a fit of rage after a fight with his wife, a man flung a cat and her litter of kittens to their death from the seventeenth floor of an apartment building and was handed a fifty-thousand-won fine; another man, who burned the eyes of at least eight puppies with a lighter, made them swallow razors, and subjected them to all sorts of atrocities, was fined a hundred thousand won. The courts imposed a sum that was little more than the price of a bottle of liquor for murdering and torturing animals. What do you think of such occurrences, Ms. Moon?

I don't believe in the law. In the end, it will always give way before men, before money, and before humans.

Unfortunately, Bell's owner was a forty-year-old woman, and poor. Meanwhile, the suspect who'd murdered Bell—who likely lived in the same neighborhood—was male. The greatest disadvantage of all was that while the victim was an animal, the assailant was human. For the injured party, entrusting the matter to the law was bound to be a losing game. The woman therefore decided not to leave it to the court. She judged it was best not to do so, even for the dead dog's sake. After receiving an apology from the suspect, she planned to forget the whole incident.

Did the woman know who the suspect was from the start? Of course not. At least, not until he turned up of his own accord.

One Sunday evening, the suspect came to see her. When she laid eyes on him, the woman was stunned. It was the same child who'd contacted her after discovering the dog's body. The boy probably told her something like this:

"I'm very sorry. It was I who killed your dog. I was riding along on my bike when I hit the dog in passing without realizing it. I thought it was just a garbage bag at first. But when I realized it was a dog, my only thought was to run away. At my age, everyone makes that kind of mistake. On the outside, they act brave, but inside, they're all just cowards. I'll accept any punishment you decide to give me."

Even as he apologized to a woman who could have been his mother, the boy didn't appear at all nervous. He seemed to her—unusually for kids these days—conscientious and resolute. The woman felt tender concern. The thought of the dead Bell made her tremble, but the suspect was close to her son in age, and when she saw how, in remorse, he'd sought her out personally, her loathing dissipated. Instead, she worried for the boy and consoled him.

"I understand. Now, off you go home. Everything will be all right."

Isn't this terribly unfair?

It was the boy who'd committed a crime, and yet he was the one being consoled. Then, who was going to console the woman? Who was going to console Bell, who had shuddered in fear before being ruthlessly murdered?

Now, I wonder—did the boy truly feel remorse for his crime?

In fact, did he even realize that he'd committed a crime?

I believe the boy must pay a price. That's what I thought then, and my feelings haven't changed since. I don't trust everything he said, either. Hit by a bicycle? If that's really what happened, the dog's cervical vertebrae wouldn't have fractured that badly. And that would mean the boy was lying—since, judging by the state of Bell's body when it was discovered, it was clear that someone had deliberately killed the dog. Even if what the boy claimed was true, further injury must have been inflicted afterward.

From his earlier encounter with her as a witness, the boy would have learned that the victim's family was a vulnerable middle-aged woman. He'd also have found out from their conversation somehow that she had a teenage son. This woman, his clever mind must have decided, will certainly forgive a boy her son's age.

Yes, he guessed correctly.

She didn't report him to the police.

He's a gifted and intelligent boy. He's bright enough not to have missed out on the top rank in his class for all three years of middle school. I heard he even competed in the International Mathematical Olympiad as a member of the national team. I've seen the prizes and certificates in his bedroom. It baffles me that such a brilliant child could have come from a household like yours.

The reason why the boy confessed must have been extremely straightforward.

I would guess he was bored. Most would call that spiteful and ill-natured.

The cruel and selfish psychology of wanting to see someone suffer. It's not hard to observe among boys his age. It's also their way of relieving stress.

But he wasn't able to anticipate what the woman did next.

Five days later, in hopes of putting an end to the boy's distress, the woman decided to speak to his parents. She thought they would be able to help him work through whatever turmoil and guilt he must be feeling inside. Yet when she went to see you, what did you say to her, Ms. Moon? Surely you haven't forgotten already? Speaking loudly so that everyone in the neighborhood could hear you, you said:

"Do you know just how clever my son is? And you're saying he killed a dog—oh, please. I know people like you very well; have us in your sights, did you, so you could fleece someone rich? Well, you failed. I'm sorry, but I'm not a pushover, to fall for your tricks. Oh, wait—I know who you are. You sell fish in the alley out front, don't you? And you have a son with an intellectual disability, right? You know what they say, sometimes kids like that can't suppress their urges; so for all we know, it could have been your own intellectually disabled son who killed Bell, or whatever the hell its name is, don't you think so? Do you have solid proof your son didn't do it? Why are you making that face? Like I'm a bad person. What, did I say something wrong? You talk about my son like he's some kind of lowlife that goes around slaughtering dogs, and you're looking at me like your son couldn't have done it. Listen to me carefully. My son will go far in life. He's going to be a mathematician representing his country. If a false rumor like this one, or worse, so much as spreads in the neighborhood and makes problems for his future, then your family won't make it out in one piece, either—remember that. You think I won't be able to do it? And I'm warning you, you'd better keep a tight leash on your son. Don't you know that kids like him commit crimes wherever they go? If you don't watch your mouth, I might make sure your son goes to jail. No, would a hospital be better? Just the fact we live in the same area as people like you and your son creeps me out and makes me feel sick. Even hearing you speak my son's name is like having sewage dumped on my body. How dare you try to blame my son for something your son did."

What do you think? Is it coming back to you now?

Surely you haven't forgotten, either, what became of that mother and son after that day?

Two days later, the woman left the gas on and died in her home beside her son. Remember how I once told you that my mother and younger brother lost their lives in an accident? Well, yes, that's the truth. Are you getting the picture now? You might wonder how someone could die for such a petty reason. But the story changes if the person had already attempted suicide. Every day, as she looked after my brother, my mother grew more and more exhausted. By the time my brother turned thirteen, she could no longer find in herself the strength to carry on and had started to entertain thoughts she should never have had. Holding on to my brother's hand, my mother leapt in front of an oncoming truck. If the driver had been looking elsewhere, or if he'd been a novice at driving, they might well have died that very same day. This traffic accident was long ago, my mother's first attempt at suicide. It's an accident that has nothing to do with you or your son.

Having come this far, I hope you aren't feeling anything remotely like guilt. If you are, I'd like you to ignore it completely. That way, wouldn't it be easier for me to maintain my hatred toward you?

For several months, I struggled with my guilt.

Why hadn't I been able to stay by my family's side? Had it really been necessary for me to room at my friend's place near the university? Wouldn't I have been able to prevent their deaths if I'd been with them?

Above all, my heart was heavy with the memory of what I'd said to my mother the day before the accident. She'd called me after hearing your vicious words, but instead of comforting her as a daughter should, I'd said to her, "Well, why did you do such a stupid thing? See what comes of caring too much about other people's business, when you could have just reported it to the police. Why did you put yourself through that?" Even in my grief, I resented her for deciding to kill herself and leave behind a scarcely college-age daughter.

But that was only for a fleeting moment, because right away I thought:

What are you and your son—who'd trampled on my family—doing right now?

In the days following the incident, my head was entirely filled with thoughts of revenge. Not even hacking your son to death in front of your eyes felt like it was going to satisfy me. No—since I'd lost my mother and my brother all at once, it would only be fair if I hacked other members of your family to pieces as well.

First, to get my revenge, I had to gain access to you.

How would I be able to enter that house? How might I be able to slowly tighten my grip around their throats? I kept going over these questions, again and again, in my mind.

You must be wondering how I was able to enter your home as a private tutor.

You'll remember Kim Minhyeok, who introduced me to you.

As you know, he's the private tutor who taught Yuchan's younger brother, Yujae, at your home for half a year until he passed the job on to me.

I had been watching your house every day, and one day I spotted a man coming out of the house. He turned out to be a senior from the same university as me. When I approached Kim Minhyeok at university and greeted him, he was very glad to see me, and I suggested we have a conversation at a nearby café. I'd worn my hair long and put on a fluttering chiffon skirt in an attempt to look demure and innocent; and, as it happened, he was into that type of girl.

After that day, we met up often and soon grew very close. The more we talked, the more we discovered that we had other things in common. Like me he suffered from insomnia, he adored cappuccinos, he couldn't handle spicy foods very well, and he loved listening to Rachmaninoff. We even shared a love of animals. He also kept two cats, he said. It wasn't long before we became involved. I'd only intended to use him when I'd made my initial approach, but little by little I'd fallen for him.

But it turned out he'd had misgivings from the start. One day, lying in bed, he told me he wanted to hear the real reason I'd approached him. I made a full and honest confession. I didn't want to hide things from him anymore, nor did I think there was any reason to. And I trusted this man would be able to understand my feelings. True to form, after listening to all I had to say, he said he'd be on my side.

Everything after that is as you know it. A month later, citing family problems, Minhyeok abruptly announced he wouldn't be tutoring anymore, didn't he? And then he introduced me to you as a trustworthy student he knew from university.

I've answered the question of how I was able to enter your home as a tutor. This should quench any remaining thirst for answers that burns inside your throat.

There are several pieces of information that Minhyeok gave me at the time, one of them being that you rarely replaced a tutor once you found one to your liking. He even wrote down for me a few things about the type of tutor you preferred.

1. Arrives ten minutes early
2. Concludes the tutorial ten minutes later than agreed
3. Does not take a break for longer than five minutes on the dot
4. Never, under any circumstances, misses a lesson
5. Does not dress too ostentatiously (← This is the most important part!)

Were you aware of this?

Of the little amount of effort I put in so I could gain your approval, for instance? I even cut my hair into a short bob for you, when I hadn't given myself an above-the-shoulder haircut since middle school, not even once.

Minhyeok also gave me a detailed description of his student, Yujae.

He'd had the impression, he told me, that the boy was smart but seemed uninterested in studying. This was despite the fact that he had a brighter mind than most children. In fact, two months ago, Yujae showed me the results of an IQ test he'd taken at his school, and he had earned a pretty high score. Do you want to know what he got? Of course you do, since he wouldn't have shown it to you. Yujae's IQ was no less than 168. The test was administered by the school so its accuracy might be somewhat suspect; but even allowing for that, the score's hardly mediocre.

Then what was going on here? Why did Yujae lose interest in studying?

It was only later that I discovered why, but the reason was that he'd lost all motivation.

When I met Yujae for the first time, I thought he looked like a boy trapped in a world of his own making. He gave off the strong impression of a teenager who didn't easily open up to others. I know children like that quite well. Outwardly, they appear to bristle like hedgehogs if you provoke them, but inside they're hoping desperately that someone will listen to them. I don't think you knew this—even though it's the most important thing.

I pitied him for having a parent who was as selfish, coldhearted, and rude as you. I wanted to rescue him from having to live under the same roof with strange people like you and Yuchan.

I was sincere in how I treated Yujae.

In response, he began to gradually open up to me. There's really no cure like attention and dialogue, it seems. We shared many conversations. We discussed a range of topics, including which foods we liked and which countries we wanted to visit. Do you know how much he came to love Albert Camus?

Do you get it now?

You were neglecting a child starved of affection.

It's said that childhood and adolescence are the most important periods in a person's life. The levels of trust and affection in a parent-child relationship during those periods greatly influence not only the development of an individual's personality but also the entire arc of the person's life. I've read articles suggesting that murderers, psychopaths, and sexual perverts turn out the way they do because of problems relating to parental affection.

Right now, you'll be growing increasingly defensive.

But I loved my children without discrimination, you'll be confidently assuring yourself. I understand. It's an illusion and a form of arrogance from which all parents suffer. As they say, however: No finger won't hurt if you bite down on it, but some fingers will hurt a little less.

Without realizing it, you will have played favorites with your children. It would have been subtle, so neither you nor Yuchan might have noticed, but Yujae would have felt it. Wouldn't it be stranger if he hadn't been able to, with an IQ of 168? Having realized he would never be able to redirect your attention away from his brother, no matter how hard he tried, he'd decided to go in the opposite direction: My mother won't take any interest in me even if I turn myself into my brother—so I might as well become a second-rate human being. He'd thought his mother would at least look his way if he acted out like this. It's a very adolescent form of reasoning. He thought that if he deliberately stopped studying and his grades dropped, his mother would take an interest in him. In the end, the child's plan worked. Just as he hoped, you hired a tutor for him.

How agonizing it must have been for him.

Pretending the ploy was going to work, though he knew it wouldn't, would have been a very difficult thing to do.

Was he tormented by these things? Is that why he turned out the way he did?

You probably can't begin to imagine why I've suddenly brought up Yujae, or the things he's done.

If I may, I'll begin by saying that you may have trusted your children too much.

As a rule, no one should be too trusting of others. What's the first thing we learn as babies? Don't trust another person for no good reason. Even your own flesh and blood to whom you gave birth is no exception. After all, one's offspring are other people, too.

Yet nowadays people trust others too easily. They open the door to anyone claiming to be the deliveryman, they're unable to refuse the pleas of a child or elderly person asking for directions, and they'll knock back any cold drink that someone hands them on a hot day. There are even some women who'll invite a traveling salesman into their homes for coffee if he happens to be good-looking. Such people fail to suspect that the other party might be exploiting their altruism, curiosity, or sexual desire — the three greatest human weaknesses. And that's because the other party is a frail, elderly person, a small child, or even a pretty youth. Both my mother, who'd taken the boy at his word, and you, who believed your child was kinder than anyone, trusted other people too easily.

I realize now that, in your case, there's one more.

Next time, don't be too trusting of private tutors, either.

To repeat what I said earlier, my desire to hack Yuchan, your eldest boy and the one who killed Bell, to death was genuinely heartfelt. So when I heard he'd had that accident, I was—I regret to say—elated. Lost his footing on a pedestrian overpass? It felt heaven-sent. But I'm human, too, and when I saw the boy lying unconscious in a coma, my resolve began to weaken. For a brief second, the sight of you weeping over your son moved me to pity.

But that's nothing.

He may be in a coma, but he's not dead yet.

It's only fair if he dies.

At least, that's what I thought, until I discovered who the real suspect was.

Early this morning, I received a text message from an unknown number.

As soon as I saw what it said, I was so shocked that for a while I couldn't take my eyes off the screen. My teeth chattered from the shock. It was as if everything I believed in was falling apart all at once. I didn't know who the sender was, but I was certain it was someone who knew about last year's events better than I did. I was also certain that the message was telling the truth. I knew with certainty. It wasn't a faint sort of inkling, this sense of certainty; it was a feeling that was far stronger and more intense than that. A woman's intuition, maybe. As a fellow woman, you must have experienced something like it, too, at least once in your life — the same feeling of disquiet you get from a sense of déjà vu.

The message included the name of the real suspect behind last year's incident.

Of course, I couldn't trust an anonymous message completely.

So I decided to question, indirectly, the "real suspect" mentioned in the text.

When I arrived half an hour before the start of our lesson, the boy was already sitting at his desk and working on his equations. He was so absorbed in his task that he didn't see me enter the room, and about five minutes went by before he finally noticed I was leaning against the door, watching him. "What are you doing?" he asked so guilelessly that I said he'd been so hard at work that I hadn't had the heart to break his concentration, and then went to sit down beside him. Lowering his head a little, Yujae pored over his workbook again, and I stared intently at his profile. I hadn't noticed it before, but he had gorgeous eyes. From the way his high nose and lips resembled yours, I guessed his slender eyes must take after his father's. Anyway, in as normal-sounding a voice as I could muster, I said:

"Apparently, someone saw your brother kill a dog. Did you know about that?"

I did not miss how, for a split second, Yujae's hand suddenly stopped moving. But instantly he was focusing his attention on his math problem. I decided to wait awhile longer.

About five minutes later, the boy spoke, his voice barely audible.

"Have you never wanted to kill anyone, miss?"

A chill ran down my spine.

It sounded like he was mumbling to himself rather than addressing another person. His voice was—how do I describe it? Would you understand if I said his voice sounded like he'd been possessed by a spirit, or was in the grip of lunacy? Actually, it might be a lot easier if you tried to imagine the voice of a seven-year-old proudly describing what he'd done. The point is that it wasn't his normal voice, the one both of us were familiar with.

"Well," I answered, trying to appear unaffected, "if I said no, that would be a lie."

"Can I tell you a secret? You'll find it interesting, too, miss."

Then he gave a sudden, snickering laugh. My blood ran cold.

"Do you really think he killed a dog? A coward like him?"

I couldn't say anything in reply.

"You know about the recent dog killings in the neighborhood, right? That was all me. Well, for some of the dogs, a few other kids were involved, too."

This was what it felt like to have your hair stand on end, I realized.

"You should be overjoyed. Since you're now the only grown-up who knows about this."

Despite feeling like I might faint at any moment, I asked him, "But why did you do those things? The animals didn't do anything wrong." He furrowed his brows in apparent disappointment and said:

"You're just like all the other grown-ups, miss. There's no living thing in this world that hasn't done something wrong, and that's because they're always giving off this rotting smell of body odor. Sometimes I get an awful headache from the smell — has that never happened to you, miss? They're all guilty of something; you can tell just by looking at them. Don't they look stupid? And more than anything, don't they look so ugly it makes you want to vomit? Out of them all, dogs look the most stupid. So stupid that just looking at them makes me boil with rage. That's a reason in itself for why they should die. I locked one up inside a fridge last winter, and it kept making a noise that was as stupid as its face. Whining, whimpering. You should have heard it, too, miss. Oh, and this is kind of interesting — did you know that everyone who owns a dog looks stupid, too? And they'll cry their eyes out over a dead animal like it's some kind of disaster. The first one I killed was owned by this middle-aged woman — oh yeah, that's right. From the fish shop. I was pretending to be my brother, and like an idiot, she really believed me."

"You didn't feel anything like a guilty conscience?"

"What did you say?"

"A guilty conscience."

"About what?"

"About what you did to those animals, their owners. And to your brother. He could have been falsely accused because of you."

He screwed up his face.

"I was only joking. Why are you being so serious all of a sudden, when it's not even a big deal? It's no fun."

And then, as if nothing whatsoever had happened, he began to work on his math problem again.

I won't bother to describe at length how I felt at that moment.

You probably think I'm lying. You'll want to believe that he couldn't have done it.

But how you feel is of no concern to me.

Some people might point to what he did and curse him: "He's worse than a dog." But I won't insult him like that. Worse than a dog? What's so criminal about a dog that people will point at a piece of human trash and say they're worse than a dog? I don't understand people who throw such insults around, even out of anger. If you're going to condemn someone, you should condemn that person alone.

It's Yujae's birthday today, I believe.

Exactly an hour ago, as our lesson came to an end, I presented him with a cake I'd brought as a birthday gift. Thanking me, he said cheesecake was a personal favorite and that he'd enjoy it. That was a relief. I had been worried he wouldn't like it. It had occurred to me only after I'd made the purchase that cheesecake could be off-putting for some because of its oily richness. But he said he was going to enjoy it, for which I was grateful.

Oh, and about that cake.

I borrowed a small amount of the potassium cyanide that — as you showed me once, some time ago — you kept stored inside the kitchen cabinet. The same potassium cyanide you said you'd procured with difficulty so you could catch and feed it to the person responsible for Yuchan's accident. As I've said before, your greatest mistake was trusting me too much.

As I was leaving, Yujae was opening the cake box, so it might all be over by now. There won't be any point in contacting me by phone or by landline. Having prepared it yourself, you'll know better than anyone how rapidly potassium cyanide takes effect. But all the same, don't blame yourself or despair too much.

Isn't it truly ironic? A birthday present becomes a parting gift.

I don't suppose you're crying over the loss of your son. Do you resent me for being too heartless?

But it can't be helped. After all, even if you resent me, I still wish with all sincerity that your heart gets slashed to ribbons.

I'm thinking of going down to Jeju Island for a while. I plan to stay at a boardinghouse and take some time off. If you have a conscience, I trust you won't do anything so foolish as to call the police.

Ah, I'll end with a couple of questions for you, too.

For what reason did Bell have to be killed by Yujae last year?

Who had the right to end that poor dog's life? Who had the right to end the lives of my mother and brother?

If Yujae was guilty of anything, it was the fact that he had a mother like you. After all, it wasn't the boy or anyone else who'd turned him into such a nasty piece of work, but you. That's the main reason Yujae had to die. Could there be a more certain and obvious reason?

But what can you do—about the fact that you're his mother, and he's your son?

Now, how are you going to answer my questions?

2.
I AM A BAD MOTHER
[JIWON'S REPLY]

How have you been, Mira?

You must have been very surprised to receive my letter. I asked Minhyeok for the address of your boardinghouse.
    The canola must be in full bloom right now on Jeju Island.
    Has it been three months? Since you left us, that is.
    Mira, are you feeling tormented by what you did three months ago? It was when I saw Minhyeok hand me your address without hesitation that the possibility dawned on me. He must have hoped I'd say these words to you, too, without fail — which only goes to show what a difficult time you must be going through at this moment.

In your letter, Mira, you said I would be confident in my belief that I loved my children without discrimination.

I'm sorry, but you're wrong.

No one discriminated more between my children than I did.

You wanted to know what Yujae was like growing up, I believe.

He was not like normal children. Unlike them, he didn't like to play with friends, and he always seemed to be lost in a world of his own. He wouldn't smile, either. I tried all manner of things to make him laugh, but he simply wouldn't smile. I started to feel depressed, too. I couldn't understand why a child, who ought to be roaring with laughter merely at the sound of his name, should be so unsmiling. What exactly had made his heart so cold? Every night I asked myself this question, but all that returned was a deafening silence.

It's true that, at the time, my husband and I were too young to understand a child like him. Worst of all, I even began to think the boy was unnatural. Despite the fact that I'd given birth to him, I felt a strange sense of detachment, as if he was someone else's child. To tell you the truth, I was afraid at first that he might be autistic, but when I took him to the hospital for an assessment, the results came back as normal.

Did this make me feel relieved, then?

Since both my husband and I knew that parents must accept and embrace their children no matter what, we never let it show in front of the boy that we were concerned. Involuntarily, however — since parents are also human — our behavior must have given away the thoughts we were harboring inside. Seeing as the boy was aware of it, that is. As you say, Mira, I might have been lost in my own false beliefs and arrogance.

At some point, I realized that the boy was jealous of his older brother.

Just as parents cannot hide the way they feel inside, neither can children. Every single expression, every single reply, holds an emotion. He must have sensed that I loved his older brother more than I loved him. Mira, didn't you say you felt guilt when your mother and brother died? How can I express in words the guilt that I, as a mother, feel when I cannot entirely deny that my child feels discriminated against by my words and actions? As if the heart is being seared with a hot iron — yes, you could say it's exactly that kind of feeling. A mother and child are connected in their hearts by a slender thread, and when the child's heart aches, so does the mother's. You wouldn't know since you're not a mother yet, but there's no relationship as mysterious and profound as that of a mother and child.

In contrast to Yujae, Yuchan was a normal, dependable child. Compared to other children his age, he had a strong sense of responsibility, he was sincere, and, as you know, he had an extraordinary head for numbers.

But there is still something you don't know, Mira.

It wasn't the older boy but the younger child who was, in fact, more intelligent.

Unlike Yuchan, who began to distinguish himself in middle school, Yujae stood apart from the rest since the day he was born. He began to walk five months earlier than the average child; he could read books from the age of three; and at age five he even memorized the world atlas. In elementary school, he won every essay contest he entered, even rousing suspicion that some grown-up had written the essays for him. In sixth grade, after picking up math by himself without once receiving private tutoring, he represented his school in a national mathematics competition. He didn't tell me that himself, of course. But there's probably not a single parent who doesn't know what is going on in their children's lives. It's my belief that parents have no choice but to know, indeed they must know, whatever situation their child is in, what their child is thinking, and what their child is going around doing. I'm sure your parents were the same, Mira.

But you consider it strange that Yujae didn't share such happy news with his mother, don't you?

As you know, Mira, it was around that time that Yuchan was selected to represent the country at the International Mathematical Olympiad. A national competition versus an international one. Yujae must have thought it inevitable that he'd be compared to his older brother once again. That's why he stayed tight-lipped. From that day on, his grades began to fall in a rapid decline. When I asked him one day why he wouldn't study, this was his reply: It's not that I'm not studying; I'm just bad at it because it's too hard.

Mira, you said you trusted a woman's intuition, yes?

So do I. To this day, my intuition has never failed me. Intuitively, I realized that the boy was lying and that he was doing it deliberately to spite me and make me feel guilty.

I'm well aware, yes. No parent will think this way just because their child has given up on studying. I know better than anyone that I'm not qualified to be a parent.

But what if this isn't the first time that your child has behaved in this way?

This might be difficult to believe, but once, to spite me, he deliberately stabbed his ear with a fork. He was only seven years old. I've also been called to his school before because of a violent incident. It was during his first year of middle school. He'd hit a girl in his class until bruises showed on her face. Unable to put up with it, the girl had appealed to the homeroom teacher for help, and the teacher thought I should be informed. But suddenly, in apparent fright, the girl apologized to me, saying that she'd hurt herself and had lied about it for her own amusement. To me, those words sounded more like an actual lie. Out of fear that my son would retaliate, she'd made up that story to make it seem as if he hadn't really hit her.

Back at home, I asked him what had happened. The girl had staged it all by herself to get his attention, my son lied. Then — would you believe it? — feigning sympathy, he said, "It's okay. I think she's had the hardest time of it." It was like receiving an electric shock. Seeing him pretend to care for a girl whom he'd struck hard enough to bruise her face made my heart tremble so much that I couldn't speak a word.

What do you think? Do I still seem like a reprehensible parent to you?

If you had been in my shoes, Mira, would things have been any different?

But the real reason I wasn't able to love that boy has nothing to do with such trivial issues.

That's right — everything I've said so far is petty and trivial compared to what I'm about to say next.

My arm is falling asleep. I'll rest for a while, then write again.

I suspect you already know, Mira.

That the children have no father, I mean. It is probably for this reason that — I don't know if you've noticed — a certain gloom pervades the house.

If I might digress a little with a tale from the past: I met my husband while we were at university. Mira, you said you liked animals. So did he. It was at an animal shelter that we first met. I was there with my friends to fulfill my volunteer hours, but he'd come out of a genuine desire to help those poor, abandoned animals. What did you dream of as a child, Mira? His dream was to rescue cats and dogs all over the country from being sold in cages. Isn't that a truly childish idea? But not all children have such dreams. I dreamed of becoming a doctor, after all.

PETTY LIES

He'd just turned twenty, he said, when he realized his childhood dream was an impossibility. It goes to show how exceptionally slow-witted and warmhearted he was as a person. His very personality was what drove him to an animal shelter every weekend. I found myself drawn to his sincerity. I knew that every time he looked after those abandoned dogs and rabbits with damaged bodies, he'd secretly retreat to a corner afterward and cry; I also knew that he went to the shelter every weekend without exception, even though on weekdays, after his classes in traditional Korean medicine, he would normally stay up long past 3 a.m. helping out at his parents' shop. He was unlike any of the countless men I knew. While those men lavished time and money on alcohol, cigarettes, cars, and women, he offered his to those in need. I'd never met anyone so pure of heart.

It wasn't just animals whom he showered with concern and affection, of course.

Women, children, disabled people, the disadvantaged, animals, and older people, he told me, were all vulnerable beings who deserved our attention. "Who's the most vulnerable of them all?" I asked one day, teasing him a little, and without missing a beat, he replied, "Young children, and then animals." Dubiously, I asked him why; until then, I'd considered disabled persons to be the most vulnerable group. He gave a quick smile, and again he didn't hesitate to reply. I still can't forget the answer he gave me. "Because they're not strong enough to protect themselves," was what I was expecting him to say. But what I heard was a completely different answer.

"Because they are purer than anyone else. Here, purity doesn't mean chastity, but rather purity of heart. Their hearts are clean, free from impurities like selfish desires and harmful thoughts, so they cannot understand violence. They don't know the very reason for the existence of violence or its definition."

And, he added, the people who inflicted harm on such children and animals were the most wicked among the wicked.

As soon as I heard those words, I knew — I'm in love with this man.

As you probably know, Mira, it's not too difficult for a person to feel sympathy for a fellow human being. You see, people are naturally predisposed to feel concern and pity for those who belong to the same group or situation as themselves. If a man strikes another man, no one thinks that the first man should be killed. What happens if a dog bites a man, however? People would waste no time in calling for the dog to be beaten to death. The same applies to older people and young children. In Korean society, under the strong influence of Confucian values, striking an older person is considered an especially unpardonable act. But what do people think of the act of striking a child? Is it as taboo as striking an older person? Whom do you think people will throw rocks at — a person who has struck an older person on the head, or someone who has done the same to a child?

I've briefly strayed off topic, I notice.

As the child of diplomats, I grew up wanting for nothing. When I was young, I spent time in Australia, the United States, Hong Kong, and Paris; I even have an Australian residency permit. My husband, by contrast, hadn't once left Korean soil. Never mind going abroad — in all twenty-seven years of his life, he hadn't even been to Jeju Island.

We'd led such different lives. So, no — in all honesty, I can't deny that I looked down on my husband's family. It's fine if you criticize me for being hypocritical. That's the kind of person I, Moon Jiwon, am. Regardless of how much I loved the man, I couldn't bring myself to accept his family. How did he react to that? Well, what do you think?

He was completely understanding. It was entirely reasonable that I'd feel this way, he reassured me. After that, Mira, how could I have loved any other man?

My husband passed away in an accident.

He died from electrocution.

A hair dryer fell into the bathtub while he was taking a bath. It was all over in a second.

You will know, I think — just how much grief is caused when you lose someone you love in the space of an instant.

When I discovered my husband's dead body, my limbs trembled as if they were caught in an earthquake. I felt like I might suffocate to death at any moment. He was lying submerged in the bathtub, and he wasn't moving.

It was terrible, bad luck. Yes, that's what I told myself at the time. That it was an accident, and that no one was to blame. No one.

But right away, doubt assailed me.

What if it wasn't a freak accident?

What if someone had deliberately caused it to happen?

And what if the person responsible was a member of the family?

You'll probably remember the Kang Ho-sun murder incident, from seven years ago.

It turned the country upside down.

The serial killer — who operated in Seocheon County, in South Chungcheong Province — had at least ten confirmed female victims. The details that emerged only added to the horror: he'd collected an enormous insurance payout by murdering his fourth wife and mother-in-law in an arson attack, and used his beloved dog as an ingredient in dog stew, and so on. But what was he like, normally? Did he look like a criminal at first glance? If he had, no one would have tried to get close to him, and no woman would have wanted to marry him, either. Yet his neighbors spoke highly of him and he married several times. How was this possible? Would the average person have been able to pull it off?

Everyone — at least once in their lives — will have entertained murderous or malicious thoughts about someone else. You have, too, and so have I. Occasionally, there'll be people whose hearts palpitate at the very thought. Simply having those emotions is enough to make them feel guilty.

But that only relates to normal, ordinary people.

People who are abnormal cannot feel guilt. Words like "sadness," "pity," and "conscience" are as strange to them as the existence of a UFO. How would you feel, Mira, if someone like that lived near you? And if that person belonged to your family?

Initially, I thought it was improbable, too. I simply couldn't imagine something so horrific could happen to me.

That night, the news program was reporting on the Kang Ho-sun incident. The police took Kang Ho-sun to the crime scene for a reenactment. In front of reporters and residents, Kang Ho-sun, handcuffed, re-created the murder scene using a mannequin of a woman. Watching it soured my mood, so I rose from my seat and withdrew to the bedroom. I was just leaning back against the pillows, about to read a book to calm my nerves, when my husband followed me inside. I noted the unusual expression on his face.

"Are you hurt somewhere?" I asked. "You don't look so well."

His ashen face was as white as a corpse. Sitting on the edge of the bed, he was silent, as if lost in thought. I watched him with worried eyes. A moment later, he spoke.

"There's something wrong with Yujae, I think."

"Why? Is he hurt? Did he catch a cold?"

"It's not like that; this is a different kind of problem."

"What could it possibly be, with you looking so grim?"

I tried nudging him with my elbow, but he didn't smile. Sometimes I'd do this during an argument, and it would make his anger dissolve like foam. I realized, then, that he was being extremely serious.

"You probably saw it, too, just now. The boy was choking the doll with his scarf, pretending to be Kang Ho-sun."

"Was he? I didn't notice."

"Don't lie to me. I know you saw it."

"So what? What about it? Kids can be like that sometimes — why are you getting so worked up about it? Talk about giving someone a fright."

"So are you saying we shouldn't be shocked by his behavior?"

"Don't be like that; the boy's just a little peculiar. Why do you keep insisting that he's abnormal?"

He made no reply.

"Don't you remember what you told me last time? Children don't know anything, you said. It's like that with him, that's all. He's only eight years old."

"This is different. He's not a child who doesn't know anything. And not every child behaves like that."

My heart felt like it was going to explode.

It wasn't that I was angry with him; I simply couldn't deny what he was saying. As I lay face down on the bed, feeling drained, he addressed me in an admonishing tone.

"I understand how you feel, but avoiding the issue won't

solve it. We need to acknowledge that he's not like other kids. And as his parents, we need to take responsibility."

What more could I say after that? If it shocked me, how much worse must it be for my husband, who held those murderers in such contempt?

He suggested that we take him to the hospital the next day to get him examined. I doubt you've heard of the PCL-R assessment, Mira. It's a test for antisocial personality disorder, and the name was new to me at the time, too. What happens if the results indicate a personality disorder, I wanted to know, and he told me the boy would have to be hospitalized and receive regular treatment. I felt uneasy as I listened to his words, but there was nothing I could do other than agree with him. I didn't want to admit that the child I'd given birth to had a personality disorder. What parent would want that?

Yes, that's right. That's certainly what I was thinking at the time.

Now, I only blame myself — why couldn't I have noticed the boy's condition sooner?

It was on that very night that my husband died.

If I hadn't seen what I'd seen, things would be very different right now.

But I did end up seeing it: my younger son saying he needed to pee, urging his father to open the door. I also knew for a fact that it hadn't been twenty minutes since the boy had last gone to the bathroom.

Had he overheard our conversation? Perhaps, perhaps not.

To be perfectly honest —

I can't say for certain whether it was the boy who caused the dryer to fall into the bathtub.

Nor can I say whether he knew you could get electrocuted if a dryer fell into the water while it was connected to an outlet.

But why did it happen on that particular day, of all days?

Why was the hair dryer — which my husband didn't normally use — lying around in the first place?

At my husband's funeral, the boy did not cry.

Was it because he was too young to know what death was? Was it for that reason alone?

My heart is trembling, so I will stop here today.

Right about now, you're thinking: Surely not.

A son killing his own father? It doesn't make any sense, you think. And an eight-year-old child at that — it makes it all the harder to believe. Well, I thought so at first, too.

I know it's not right for a mother to have such suspicions. I deserve to be rebuked for being not in my right mind. How can a woman suspect not just anyone but her own son? But I think you will be able to understand me, Mira. Why I was seized by the same anxiety that later gripped you. Why I was driven to the point of suspecting my own child.

After that incident, I began to avoid him even more.

His eyes were especially painful to look at. Every time I glimpsed those eyes, which — as you guessed, Mira — resembled his father's, I'd be reminded of my husband, and it would cause me so much anguish I could hardly bear it. Perhaps for this reason I grew even more dependent on and obsessed with my older son. Whenever I returned home from work, I'd always look for him first. I knew Yujae felt that he was being treated differently, but I couldn't help it.

It was around that time that your mother came to see me.

She explained to me, regretfully, what my older son had done. I'd already worked out what was going on, however. Only my younger child could have done something so heinous. But why did she think it was Yuchan? More importantly, how did she know which school he attended?

In that instant, my intuition was telling me — this was, without a doubt, a scheme of Yujae's.

Just as he'd done to his father, the boy was intending to plunge his brother into the depths of hell.

Unhappily, however, I could no longer afford to humor him. He was starting to frighten me. I wanted to erase the fact that I'd given birth to him from my mind. I wanted to erase his existence from the world.

I'm sorry, Mira, but this much is true: your mother got caught in the cross fire.

My irritation had grown out of control. I couldn't stand the sight of this woman who had blindly accepted Yujae's claims, though I knew well enough that she was a blameless victim ensnared in his plot. Perhaps her appearance awoke the rage that was lying dormant within me. And so, quite inadvertently, I ended up unleashing a torrent of abuse at her. When I saw her face turn white, I was filled with regret, but by then it was too late. Feeling ashamed, I told her I had to be at the office, and fled the scene.

If there are two things I regret most bitterly right at this moment, the first is that I didn't promptly seek treatment for the boy after my husband's death; the second is how wickedly I behaved to your mother and brother. And to you, too, of course.

Mira, when you came to us on Minhyeok's recommendation, I genuinely could not believe my eyes.

Did you think I didn't know who you were?

But of course I did. I recognized you the moment I laid eyes on you.

You may not know this, but as a matter of fact I went to your mother's wake last year. Does this surprise you very much? Actually, I felt guilty for saying such harsh words to your mother that day. So, I went to the fish shop where she worked. Even though it was a weekday afternoon, the shop was closed. I went back the next day, but the shop was still closed. Curious, I asked people working at nearby stores, and they told me that your mother passed away the day before due to an unfortunate incident. I asked them for the funeral details, and fortunately, they knew and told me.

A young woman was standing there who looked just like her, so I gathered she was the woman's daughter. I was too ashamed to face you at the time, Mira, and returned straight home. Afterward, I wanted to help you in any way I could but was at a loss, since I didn't know your address or your number.

And then you showed up right in front of me, Mira. And on Minhyeok's recommendation, no less.

What an astonishing coincidence!

But I don't believe in coincidence.

I knew there had to be a reason you suddenly appeared before me. It wasn't difficult to guess that the reason would be revenge. I would have felt more or less the same way, after all. There's not a single person who wouldn't be furious after losing their family in the space of an instant.

You assumed that the past year would be hazy in my mind, didn't you? You're quite wrong. Like you, Mira, I remember the events of that day vividly, like they happened yesterday. How can I forget, when someone died because of me?

When I asked you about your family, Mira, you told me your father had passed away from an illness when you were little, and that your mother and brother had died in an accident not long ago. You might have tried to conceal it, but I could feel it — the hostility in your eyes as you gazed at me. Remorse and guilt swept over me. I wanted to pull you into a hug that very second, Mira.

But at once I was struck by the following thought:

Mira thinks my older son is responsible for last year's incident. Therefore it is not Gong Yujae, but Gong Yuchan against whom she holds a grudge.

My thought was to protect that blameless child. Yet I couldn't bring myself to tell you the truth. Even if you did learn the truth, I told myself, nothing would change. It wouldn't change the fact that, a year ago, I'd killed your mother and brother.

So I'm telling you this now, Mira, but I secretly asked Minhyeok to keep an eye on you. I thought he'd refuse, but to my surprise he readily accepted my request. Could it be that, on the surface, he was acting as if he was committed to helping you when in fact he was hoping, inwardly — like me — that you'd put your revenge on hold?

I'm sorry if this offends you. But I'd like you to understand that there was nothing else I could do. If it's for my older son, I am capable of doing anything. If it keeps him alive, I can even kill a person. I am prepared to do worse. It's fine if you think me selfish. For that child, I can become the devil himself.

To my relief, Yujae appeared to like his new tutor. In fact, he seemed to be opening up more with you than he had with Minhyeok, which I found reassuring.

Do you know the real reason why I made him receive home tutoring, Mira?

I needed someone other than myself who could teach and supervise him closely. I wanted to give him another parental figure. I was hoping someone else, in my stead, would do what I'd been unable to do. And most of all, during the tutorials at least, the boy wouldn't be able to go astray. I always felt uneasy about what he might be getting up to outside the home. That was why I wanted to keep him indoors for as long as possible. In the past he'd have been flatly opposed to the idea of having a private tutor, but this time, for whatever reason, he agreed without protest. I was overjoyed. For the first time, I felt that he might be changing.

The old adage — as children grow older, they change twenty times over — was right. Before long, the boy was starting to behave like other children. Like a normal child, he'd return from school on time, and after lessons he'd hang out with friends or study by himself in his room. Sometimes he'd bring his friends over for a chat or to play games on the computer. His best friend was a levelheaded and dependable boy named Dong-gyu, who'd been made class monitor. My son, friends with a boy like him! I was deeply moved. I regretted mistaking his involvement in my husband's death. It seemed like I'd been too hard on him. Parents should believe in their children. As a mother, I'd acted badly. Feeling apologetic, I tried to be good to him.

Everything was changing — the boy, myself, even the air of heavy gloom inside the house.

Yes.

Until that happened.

• • •

At around 9:40 one Saturday night, I received a phone call saying that my older son had been in an accident.

I'd just been about to head home from work.

The news I received from the hospital — that he'd fallen down the steps of a pedestrian overpass — came as a shock, but it also made me suspicious. A pedestrian overpass? As far as I knew, there was no such structure anywhere near our house or the boy's school. When I asked for the location, they said it was the overpass in front of C Elementary School. I'd heard that the overpass is as high as six meters. What on earth had led him there? Had something happened late at night that had suddenly required him to visit the school? Or was there some business he'd needed to take care of at the nearby supermarket? What kind of scenario would call for an eighteen-year-old boy to take care of some business at a supermarket?

That night was a Saturday.

It was on a Saturday that Yuchan would come home from the school dormitory every week.

Normally, as soon as his afternoon classes were over, he would come straight home without stopping elsewhere. At around 6 p.m. — which was when he'd arrive home — I would call the house landline and he'd always pick up. Then he'd rest or study in his room until I got back from work. Never in two years had he broken this pattern. The boy I knew was as regular as clockwork. A boy like that had decided that day to go somewhere he'd never usually go. And it was there that he'd lost his footing and ended up getting into an accident.

What do you make of this, Mira? Do you think this was all a coincidence?

As I said earlier, I don't believe in coincidences. I had a sour feeling that began to bubble in my stomach. To get a more accurate grasp of the situation, I needed clues. I couldn't simply leave it to the police. They'd determined that the accident was caused by the individual's own negligence. I wanted to ask my older son what had happened, but he was in a coma and unable to communicate. It was impossible to investigate any further, they claimed, because CCTV hadn't been installed at the top of the overpass. I was dumbfounded.

Is every incident that takes place at a pedestrian overpass an accident caused by one's own negligence? In all the world, is there a more irresponsible statement?

I decided to investigate the entire area myself.

I looked inside every single shop that looked out onto the overpass. In addition to a café, there was a laundry, a convenience store, a hardware store, and a piano academy. I entered the café and sat by a window that offered the best view of the overpass. Charmingly decorated, it was the kind of café that teenagers these days found appealing. It was a cozy café with a blend of white and wood tones. The spacious interior was adorned with stylish furniture and posters radiating a retro vibe, casually hung here and there. As soon as I stepped into the café, I thought, This is the kind of place the younger generation would like. A woman in her thirties approached me with a menu. She turned out to be the café's owner. When I questioned her about the night of the accident, she said, apologetically, that she hadn't seen anything because she'd been out at the time. Then she began to question me in turn, wanting to know exactly why the boy had fallen down the overpass. Discouraged, I left after paying for my coffee and went to visit the shops next door, but there wasn't a single person who knew anything about what had happened that night. I grew disheartened. Finding a witness was not as easy as I'd expected.

Clutching at my last scrap of hope, I entered the laundry. As it happened, there was a middle-aged couple who appeared to be in their fifties. Thankfully, they looked kind. When I asked them about that night, the woman spoke first.

"Of course I remember," she muttered as she did the ironing. "How can you forget something like that? Fell down the steps of the overpass, he did, while horsing around with a friend, from the looks of it. Anyway, kids these days — they have no sense of caution."

"Get your facts straight," interrupted the man, who had been listening quietly. "The way I saw it, he was by himself!" "Again with that story!" she shouted furiously. "There were clearly two of them. Do you always have to say the opposite of whatever I say? We were enemies in a past life, that's obvious enough. Oh,

I've had it up to here with you." Then they started arguing, so I had to run out of there at once. Feeling perturbed, I was walking past the café when the owner hurried out and nervously called me over.

"Thank goodness. I was worried you might have left already. My employee said she witnessed the boy fall that night while clearing up the table by the window."

She gestured toward a very young-looking woman standing beside her. Staring at the floor, the young woman — who seemed barely twenty years old — began to mumble, her face stricken with fright.

"I was clearing the empty cups from the table when a student suddenly got up from his seat. I was surprised, so I found myself following his gaze, and that's when I saw the boy had collapsed on the ground."

"The boy who fell from those steps — was he alone, by any chance, or was he with someone else?"

"Well…"

"Try your best to remember," I implored with clasped hands. "Please."

The employee bit down lightly on her thumbnail. "Now that I think about it," she ventured, "it was dark, so I can't promise anything, but I think there was someone beside him. Yeah, that's right, there really was someone there. It was probably a girl. She was wearing a skirt, you see."

Mira —

That night, on the pedestrian overpass, Yuchan hadn't been alone.

Someone had been with him.

And that person had deliberately tried to kill him.

I'd discovered that he hadn't been by himself that night on the overpass, but I had no idea what to do next. Eventually, I decided to ask my older sister for help.

"I understand you're going through a difficult time. But doesn't that still seem like a lot of speculation?"

The somberness of her tone conveyed itself perfectly through the phone. I explained to the best of my ability what the café employee and the couple at the laundry had witnessed. Despite my efforts, her response remained lukewarm.

"You heard it yourself. The police said it was an accident caused by Yuchan's negligence. Have the police ever said anything lightly? Have a bit of faith in the Korean police. Actually, no, you should just accept what I tell you: the boy lost his footing because it was dark. So stop being so stubborn, and just keep praying that he'll wake up as soon as possible. That's the only thing you can do for that child, all right? Anyway, I hope you find my words even a little bit helpful."

My sister's words did not help in the slightest. I realized then that even siblings are no use in times like these.

I know my child best.

It wasn't the police or his aunt who had kept close watch over the boy all these years, but me, his mother. Only I knew that he wasn't the kind of child who would be so absent-minded as to lose his footing in the dark. If my son, the boy I knew, had judged it too dark to see the stairs, he would most assuredly have held on to the railing as he descended. I wanted to ask my older son what had happened, but as I mentioned earlier, he was in a coma and unable to communicate.

But these thoughts did little to help solve the problem. They only hindered me.

I put forward a hypothesis: What if?

What if the boy had been distracted? And therefore it was true that he'd lost his footing?

Still, I could not allow it.

No — I could not condone it. The very situation was impossible to condone.

In that case, what had that girl — the one who'd been with him — been up to?

Why hadn't she been able to hold on to Yuchan as he fell? Had she realized too late that he was falling? Is that why, out of fear, she hadn't even called 119 and had run away instead, abandoning him where he lay on the ground? If she'd reported the incident, surely we could have at least prevented him from falling into a coma.

My anger would not subside.

It's the same with CCTV.

If only cameras had been installed at the overpass, we could have found out the exact details of the accident — what had happened, who had been with him. The incident made me acutely aware of just how inept the government was at everything it did. How could anyone feel secure about raising a child in this country? Mira, did you know that the rate of crime on a pedestrian overpass is surprisingly high? An overpass might seem safe because it's open to the public view, but it has a significant drawback in that if you encounter a criminal, there's nowhere to run to or call for help. The crime rate is mostly made up of sexual offenses, so women, especially, should refrain as far as possible from using them. Take this warning to heart, Mira.

Have you ever heard of the city of Rockhampton in Australia? The construction of a multimillion-dollar pedestrian overpass in this small city with a population of just over eighty thousand caused a stir. Even more surprising was the fact that there was nothing in the vicinity except a private high school. It was for the sake of the students' safety alone that they'd invested such a considerable sum of money. You must be wondering what kind of overpass would cost millions of dollars to build. It was the price of installing CCTV everywhere to prevent the overpass from turning into a den of teenage delinquents and to prevent crimes from being furtively committed on top of it. It all makes me feel quite glum. I know it's no use comparing this country with a developed nation, but I keep doing it anyway. When will this habit ever go away?

By now you must be thinking that I've lost my mind from shock. As with my husband earlier, I must seem to you like someone with strange fancies about simple accidents. Who else is there to blame, you'll be berating me, when my son hadn't properly checked to see where he was placing his feet?

But, Mira.

What if he hadn't crossed the overpass willingly?

What if the girl had taken him there knowing he was in no condition to walk on top of the bridge?

I'll say this once more, but I am in an extremely normal state of mind. If you hear what I'm about to say, you, too, will understand why I couldn't think any other way.

My older son cannot cross a pedestrian overpass.

And that is because he has a terrible fear of heights.

How about that? Do you still think it was a simple accident?

Now you will be wondering, too. About the identity of the girl.

Who exactly was she? What kind of relationship did she have with Yuchan, to know about his fear of heights?

You may have worked this out already, but it was something only our family knew. He didn't want anyone finding out that he had acrophobia. However many times I tried to console him by saying he wasn't the only one with the condition, he seemed to think he suffered some kind of incurable disease and would be ashamed of it. That's why he made a point of not venturing anywhere near a high place. He simply didn't want to create a situation that required him to climb somewhere high up. At amusement parks, he wasn't able to look properly at rides like the Viking, let alone ride them.

And you're suggesting a boy like that intended to cross an overpass? He'd have searched for a pedestrian crossing, even if it took him a roundabout way. He was that kind of boy, and more.

Moreover, would he have simply told someone about this defect of his when he so hated the idea of others finding out about it? If some people like to flaunt their neuroses and others don't, he belonged squarely in the latter group. Even if a knife was pressed to his throat, he wouldn't have breathed a word of it. Who was this girl, then, who did know about it? Were they dating? Did she know because she was his girlfriend?

That, too, is impossible.

As far as I know, he didn't have a girlfriend. How could he be dating a girl when he didn't have a girlfriend in the first place? The boy couldn't even talk to girls properly. Unlike his younger brother, whose good looks always made him popular with the girls, Yuchan would run away from them. There's a difference, I believe, between ignoring the opposite sex and not being able to approach them. If his younger brother belonged to the former camp, he belonged to the latter. His interests lay solely in studying.

Even if there's a one-in-a-million chance — though it's still highly unlikely — that a boy like him really was dating a girl, the result would be the same. Is there any boy stupid enough to blurt out his shortcomings to his first girlfriend? And I'm talking about a highly sensitive boy in the full swing of adolescence. If this neurosis was something he wanted to keep hidden, he'd have tried all the harder to conceal it. Anyone would have felt the same way. That's just human nature.

Mira, I trust you are persuaded by everything I've set out so far.

In which case there can be only one conclusion.

1. The suspect, who knew my older son's weaknesses, paid the girl to encourage her to commit the crime.
2. The girl would have enticed my son by any means possible to cross the overpass.
3. The suspect chose a girl because he was male and wanted to evade suspicion.
4. Only family members know about his condition.
5. There are only two people in the family.

You'll have caught on by now, Mira.

I truly am the most infuriatingly pathetic person.

Why had I indulged in such idle notions?

Why had I assumed my younger son was changing, though I knew full well that was impossible?

If I hadn't been so lazy, my older son wouldn't have ended up like this. I wasn't able to protect him from his younger brother. I am a pathetic, stupid, bad mother.

Well acquainted with his older brother's weaknesses, the boy must have decided to make use of them.

Acrophobia, and girls.

He must have grabbed any girl at his school and urged her to do his bidding. I don't know exactly how he went about it, but he'd have used money or his looks. After all, those two things by themselves are enough to win over a teenage girl.

The girl who'd agreed to be his accomplice would have then embarked on a love-bombing operation against my older son. The love bombing wouldn't have been genuine, of course. Having never properly talked to a girl before, the boy would have fallen for it at once. I know very well just how pure and innocent my son is. The girl suggests that they start a real relationship; unopposed to the idea, he accepts. Their first date is at a café. The choice of location would have been hers. There's a café she likes to frequent, which she recommends. At 8 p.m., they meet on the street opposite. "We need to cross the road here to get to the café." The girl proposes that they cross the pedestrian overpass. Yuchan has a fear of heights, but he doesn't want to draw her attention to it. And somehow, it seems like he might be able to do it as long as he doesn't look down. Crossing the bridge doesn't seem to be an issue. The problem is going down the stairs. Suddenly, he would have had the sensation of his legs giving way, of falling bodily down the steps. No doubt he'd have experienced darkened vision and shortness of breath. Right at that moment, standing behind him, the girl would have shoved her hands against his back.

What do you think of my conjectures?

It's hard enough for normal people to regain their balance after getting pushed down a flight of stairs; how much worse must it have been for the terrified boy? I can't sleep at night at the thought of it without taking sleeping pills.

Of course, the younger child wouldn't have anticipated that his brother would go into a coma. He must have thought things would end with just a broken bone. After all, that would have been enough to torture me.

It was on the following night that I grew more certain about my conjectures.

Arriving home after work, I discovered several pairs of sneakers scattered haphazardly near the front entrance. Over by the younger boy's bedroom, a loud commotion was audible through the door. I gave a knock, but when there was no response, I simply pushed the door open and went inside. Arcade noises blasted my ears. There were about five of them inside the room. Catching sight of me, one exclaimed, "Oh! Hello?" It was the boy I knew well — Oh Dong-gyu, the class monitor. At his outburst, the other boys turned together to stare at me. From the looks on their faces, they seemed to regard me as an intruder. They gave a grudging hello before fixing their attention once more on the game. My son wasn't there. I closed the door and went to the living room.

"When did you come home, Umma?" my son called out from behind me just then.

He was holding a bottle of orange juice and some castella cake that he'd been about to take back to his room and share with his friends.

"A moment ago.... Have you had dinner?"

"I'm going to make do with this. Oh, and is it okay if my friends stay the night?"

As I simply stood there, the boy gave a slight smile and then went inside his room.

It had been barely two days since his older brother's accident.

Is it normal for a boy to invite his friends over and play games on the computer when his older brother is lying in a hospital ward, deep in a coma? Had I given birth to a person or a demon?

That was when I realized.

The boy hadn't been attempting to plunge his older brother into a living hell — the real target had been me.

This was his revenge. He must have despised me for wanting to have him hospitalized. No doubt that is also why he killed my husband. He'd kept me alive, but so he could keep me struggling in a swamp of misery. I railed against the heavens. Why did I have to give birth to a child like him and suffer such pain? Why me, of all people?

But what can you do?

As you said yourself, Mira, he was my son, to whom I'd given birth, and I was his mother.

So he could put my mind at rest, my younger son had played the role of an ordinary son. Taken unawares, I'd fallen for it. It's clear that the child has never been normal for a day in his life. Vigilant, he'd lain in wait for any opportunity to torment me. By destroying something I valued and held most dear, he'd hoped to see me suffer. He must have believed that if he wrecked his brother's life, I'd weep tears of blood.

His expectations proved correct. I did weep tears of blood. Even now, whenever I think about how my older son ended up like that because of me, my heart feels like it might split in two.

I've said it already. If it's for my firstborn son, I'm capable of doing anything.

Initially I considered killing Yujae and then killing myself. But I realized that if I died, no one would be left to care for Yuchan, and I couldn't possibly let that happen. In that case, I thought, I'll kill Yujae, and then pay for my crime for the rest of my life. I'll live a life of service and repentance.

But that wasn't so easy, either.

I couldn't find the courage to emerge unscathed after killing the child with my own hands. It was like walking barefoot on the snow. Eventually, I couldn't see a way out of this problem. I despaired. Reality was too hard and unwieldy to shoulder alone. I even resented my husband for dying ahead of me. If he were still alive, I wouldn't be suffering so much. Deep down, I prayed and prayed again. If only someone would help me. If only someone would take away this pain and heavy burden.

At that moment, it was you, Mira, who came to mind.

Mira would be able to help me, I thought. I'm sorry for making such a one-sided decision. That's why I decided to leave as much of it as possible to your discretion. I only played the part of the guide. It was I who sent you that anonymous message. With things being the way they were, I believed you at least had to know the truth. I wanted to clear poor Yuchan's name, too.

I didn't think for a moment that you'd take the message at face value. Still, I was expecting you to take action to verify its claims. From the way you behaved, I could tell without much difficulty that you had a cautious personality. And despite your youth, you showed remarkable discernment and decision-making ability. I believed you'd quickly be able to grasp that the younger boy was the suspect behind last year's incident. I hadn't expected, however, that he'd disclose with so much pride what he'd been up to.

Frankly, it would be a lie if I said I wasn't shocked by what I read in your letter. That boy was even more abominable than I'd realized. I learned for the first time through your letter that the recent dog killings in the neighborhood were all his doing, too. He'd gone around with his friends doing such horrific things. I feel sick just thinking about it. I knew he'd been pretending to be ordinary, but I'd never dreamed he would do something like that. What parent would imagine such a thing of their offspring?

Perhaps it was a blessing in disguise. What little guilt remained within me evaporated as soon as I found out. Looking back, I now know Yujae blamed that poor dog's death on his brother simply to spite me and Yuchan. That's just who he is, by nature. He should never have been born.

The day after I read your letter, I reported the five other boys to the police. Immediately, warrants were filed for their arrest and the boys were booked without detention. Now it's just a matter of time before the warrants are issued. Those boys may be in their teens, but if they've committed a crime, they should be punished for it. Needless to say, their parents were desperately denying the facts to the bitter end. They had no sense of shame. It was like seeing the way I used to be, which gave me a strange feeling. They'll have to realize, too, as soon as possible, that parents are responsible — a priori or a posteriori — for 90 percent of their child's wrongdoing.

Oh, I almost forgot the most important part.

There's one more thing I need to tell you.

You remembered where I'd kept the potassium cyanide. I was worried you wouldn't.

Now do you understand?

The person who killed that boy wasn't you, Mira; it was me. All you did was simply follow the trail of breadcrumbs I'd left for you. So there's no need to blame yourself. And try to erase the events of that day from your memory. It will be for your own good. That's what I've been wanting to tell you.

Today, Yuchan was discharged from the hospital.

Since regaining consciousness two months ago, he's been receiving regular rehabilitation treatment, and now he's much recovered. He's not quite as he used to be, but I trust he'll improve day by day. The boy isn't so feebleminded as to fall apart on the spot.

We'll be leaving for Australia next month. I plan to close down the interior business by the end of the week, too. We're thinking of brazenly imposing on my sister's generosity at her home in Melbourne. Staying in Korea will only remind us of bad times. I can't say with any certainty when we'll be returning. For the time being, I doubt there will be any reason for us to return.

Do I regret killing that boy?

Yes, I do. Enough to be plagued by nightmares every night.

Even if I were to go back in time, though, I'd do it all over again. You would, too, Mira.

I hope this has sufficiently answered your questions.

3.
I AM A GOOD SON
[YUJAE'S SITUATION]

My maternal uncle speaks; his tongue is speckled.

"Still doing well at school? Kids who do well at the start continue to do well; that's how it is. Naturally, you'll be aiming for medical school. You're going to study math at S University? So you have zero interest in medicine. I'm not saying this because I'm a doctor, but whatever the case, there's nothing like being a doctor in this country. You get paid good money, you're well respected, and you get to play all the golf you want. Hang on a minute, what was the name of your younger brother again? Isn't he still in elementary school? What, he's in his first year of middle school? How time flies. Since when was he in middle school?"

My maternal aunt speaks, her cheek twitching.

"Do you know what your baby cousin said yesterday when his

homeroom teacher asked him what kind of hero he wanted to be when he grew up? Well, he told her he wanted to be like his hyung Yuchan. The teacher asked him who that was, and apparently he said, 'It's my older cousin, and he's super clever.' Isn't that so cute? What does he know, he's only ten years old. So what did I tell him? 'Don't worry, when you get older you'll be a hundred times cleverer than Yuchan.' Because who knows? It might really happen. But this teacup is so pretty. Is it okay if I take it with me?"

My paternal uncle speaks with narrowed eyes.

"A man must strive to perfect his character. As Confucius said, at fifteen I set my heart on learning, at thirty I established the fundamentals of learning, at forty I suffered no confusion in my judgment, and at fifty—what was it again…? Anyway, what that means is, Confucius didn't study so he could rise and advance in the world; it means he set his heart on the kind of learning that would cultivate his character. How do I have all of this memorized? Don't look down on me just because I only have a high school degree. Remember, the substance of a man isn't measured by the length of the straps on his satchel. And what that means is, being a good person should come before being a good student. Does that make sense to you? Well, you're a clever boy, Yuchan, so you'll be able to get what I'm trying to say. It's those louts who won't pick up a book that can't seem to figure stuff out. What? You're Yujae? Where's your brother gone off to, then? Like peas in a pod, you two."

My paternal aunt bares a long front tooth.

"They say bluefish is good for you when you're preparing for exams. Why, apparently it's rich in omega-3 fatty acids, so it helps improve your memory. A freshman in high school these days is practically an exam candidate, you know. I hope you're not feeding him things like coffee to keep him awake, are you? That's like giving him poison. Don't forget, dear sister-in-law — our brother might have died early, but it doesn't change the fact that that boy is the first son of the first son in our family. Oh yes, was Yuchan's shirt size 95? What? He's certainly grown a lot. I was expecting him to grow one size bigger than last year since he's at that age when they shoot up. Anyway, I've bought him some clothes, but can you believe I forgot to bring them with me today? I'll send them to you next time. Oh, and let's see, there was the younger boy, too, wasn't there? Well, maybe he can wear them after Yuchan, but I'll leave that up to you. What good is having a sibling, if not for that. The boy's a bit bigger than him? Oh well, what can you do. He can't wear them, then. What's he trying to do, growing bigger than his older brother? He's just barely started middle school."

A bubble. I was always a bubble.

A precarious bubble, one that might pop anytime a finger hovered nearby. How can a person be a bubble? I used to doubt it, too. I hate words like "bubble." There's not a single decent expression featuring them. A bubble economy; foam at the mouth; skim off unwanted scum, and so on.

It's like they especially coined the phrase "unwanted scum" with me in mind. Skim off unwanted scum. Skim off, skim off, skim off. Because people don't want me; they remove me from their sight and their memories. In this way, irrespective of my will, I'm always being popped, with a pop, pop.

But that's only inside their minds. I'm not actually the one being popped; it's them. I pop them right in front of me — pop, pop. Oh, what fun it is, to pop my uncle's tongue, my aunt's cheek, my uncle's eye, my aunt's front tooth.

Do they know they're being erased from existence by someone? If they don't, I want to tell them. About how miserable it is. And how horrific.

No one cares how old I am, what school I go to, how tall I am, and what shade of skin I have, whether I'm introverted or extroverted. To them, I'm just a smaller boy that's tacked on to my brother. They don't even know my name. The other day, my paternal uncle looked straight at me and said, "Gong Yujin, don't just stand there, bring me a glass of cold water." I felt like retching. "My name's Yujae, not Yujin! You stupid old man!" I wanted to shout, but I held myself back and spat in the glass before I brought it to him. Then I smiled as I watched the water glug down his throat. As I watched my uncle, Yuchan was watching me. He stared at me with his usual expression. With dull eyes that held no emotion.

That's when it occurred to me.

Those people aren't what I want to pop, most of all.

PETTY LIES

Those cursed eyes of his. Eyes that resemble the eyes of our aunt, our mother's favorite sibling.

I take after my dad's side of the family. I know Umma doesn't think highly of them. I'd be a half-wit if I didn't know that. She's always insulting them right in front of me. "Your father's side of the family comes from a beggar neighborhood. They have low standards; they're not good enough." Yap, yap. It's so much noise. I don't particularly want to hear any of this stuff, since if I resemble my dad, it means she can't stand the sight of me, either. Does Umma hate me? If she doesn't hate me, why does she say these things to me? How come she won't say them in front of my brother? People say we look like twins, but why am I the only one who resembles our dad's side of the family?

I want to pop them like bubbles. Yuchan's eyes. And someone else's.

My mother's eyes, which become loving only when they land on my brother.

"So you're Yuchan's younger brother? You seem clever. Are you good at studying, too?"

"Is your hyung really the top student in his year? How come you aren't?"

"I don't know if I'll get into a science high school. Want to skip class and go to a PC bang? A game's just been released and apparently it's fucking brutal!"

Top of the class, top of the class. When I was little, I used to think this was some kind of amazing feat. Throughout middle school, my brother never failed to rank top of his class. Umma always told him, "It's like I was born into this world to give birth to you." Something she never said to me.

It started in elementary school, during sixth grade. The homeroom teacher must have eaten something weird because at some point she began to make us take pop quizzes. Each test consisted of ten fairly difficult questions that a middle school student might have been able to solve. Dealing with them turned out to be surprisingly easy. If there was a question you didn't understand, you could just draw a star beside it without having to work it out. It got to the point where the tests could have been mistaken for an art exam since more than half the class were scribbling only stars on their sheets. The teacher didn't seem to have expected much from the start and looked nearly ready to give up.

While some kids researched how to draw prettier stars, a few others were answering the questions so perfectly that you'd think a real middle school student had done it. There weren't many of them, but the fact they existed got on my nerves. They knew how to do something I didn't — those blockheads, who normally lagged behind me. The teacher gave them outright preferential treatment. If they had the slightest temperature, she'd force them to go home early, even if they didn't want to. If one of them forgot to bring supplies, she'd even let them use hers, demonstrating both magnanimity and the scarlet of her gums.

I didn't like math. I just didn't like playing around with numbers. But I liked Korean literacy classes. Every year, at the local essay-writing contest organized by the city of Bundang, I took home the grand prize fair and square. Back then, the privilege of leaving school early and borrowing the teacher's supplies whenever I wanted was granted only to me. But now the teacher wouldn't even look at me. It had taken barely three months. At that moment, I realized that whatever subject one had to excel at in Korea, it wasn't going to be the Korean-language area. That stuff was of no use whatsoever. It was on account of people skilled in math and English that the world went around, anyway.

My insides are twisting. So are the faces of my conceited classmates and the face of that woman, the teacher whose sweet smiles are meant only for them.

I want people to tell me, "That's my boy!" I want to hear from that woman's lips, "I had no idea you were so good at math, too! You said you wanted to go to a science high school, right? I assure you, you'll get in, absolutely."

And if Umma hears about it...

Anyway, how do I make this happen?

It was one headache of a problem. I didn't want to go to a hagwon if my life depended on it. Only blockheads go there. Hagwons are where idiots sit in rows, their mouths hanging open, staring at the chalkboard with glassy eyes. People who go around saying, "Sorry, I have to go to the hagwon," are the most pathetic lot on the planet. I don't know why anyone with half a brain would willingly go somewhere that will give them brain rot. Having no other option, I decided to ask my older brother, who was in middle school, for help. Without batting an eye, however, he said,

"You're not a little kid anymore. Don't rely on me for everything — try giving it a go by yourself first. If it's still a problem, I'll help you then."

What a joke. Like I'll ever ask you for help again.

In the end, the only person I can trust is myself. Life is lived alone, after all; there's no choice but to manage on your own.

On my way home from school, I went to a bookstore and bought myself a teach-yourself textbook and exercise book for middle school math. Once I had a rough grasp of the Pythagorean theorem and other formulae, I learned all the sample questions by heart, in a process that took no longer than four hours. When I tried getting up from my chair, my stiffened hips cracked loudly as they straightened. How much time would my brother have taken? Suddenly, the fact I'd taken as long as four hours filled me with unbearable shame. He'd have been done with everything in two hours, in exactly half as much time. That was the kind of person he was and more. At the thought, my face grew hot, as if singed by fire.

I want to win. I want to shock him.

I received eighty points on my next math test. It was up to thirty points higher than my last score. From then on, the homeroom teacher began to take notice of me, and by the time my score rose to one hundred, two weeks later, she was completely on my side. On her recommendation, I joined a group of students preparing for a math competition that was taking place in mid-July. After that, I fell headlong into the world of math. Whenever I solved a formula in under a minute, a spark from deep within me that I'd never felt before would rise and then explode like fireworks in front of my eyes. When my name was selected as the most promising student out of the eight in the group, I thought to myself: I'll take my brother down a peg this time. The news spread at the speed of light, and before long I was being called a math prodigy in the teacher's room. Math prodigy. I liked it.

My name was included in the roster of three students selected to represent the school in the national math competition. It was the only rightful outcome. I got back a little early and solved math problems while waiting for Umma to come home from work. Yuchan arrived at 8 p.m., and Umma about two hours later. I went up to her with a look of elation on my face. Deep down, I wanted to tell her the happy news immediately, but I kept my patience and waited until she took off her shoes. After all, the longer the wait, the sweeter the surprise.

"Has something good happened to you?"

Umma wore a look of mingled curiosity and anticipation; she seemed to have inferred from my face that something was up. Now I just had to speak loudly enough so Yuchan could hear me from his room.

"Actually, at school today—"

"Is your brother in his room?"

I scowled. She's always looking for my brother. Even when I'm right there in front of her, she looks for my absent brother. I'm the one who comes out to greet her at the front door, but she looks for my brother, who's shut up in his room and doesn't even bother to show his face.

"He's studying in his room."

"I'm sure. He must be hungry."

Umma was about to walk past me but turned around.

"What were you trying to tell me, earlier?"

"Well, it's about the math competition. At the—"

"Oh, I already heard about it, from your brother."

He knew about it? But how? I hadn't said anything to him.

"You were about to tell me that he's going to the international math competition, weren't you? Isn't it just so impressive? Not even the national level—he's representing the country at the international level. There are six of them in the group and he's the only one in middle school. Now you can brag all you want to everyone about how great your brother is."

It felt like the roof was caving in. In that moment, something inside me split into two, like a fish being cleaved in half by a kitchen knife.

I'm afraid.

I'm afraid that it's not just in my imagination and that I'm actually a bubble. I'm scared that, like a bubble, I might actually burst.

That person — who, ever since he was born, has been one step ahead of me, who monopolizes Umma's love and pride, and whom I can never overtake.

I want to do it.

I want to burst that thing that is my brother. Explode! Go away! Disappear!

But I know. Realistically, so long as the ground doesn't cave in, it's not possible.

Wait a minute — why can't I make it happen? If the ground doesn't cave in on its own, surely I can force it to.

That's it, I make him disappear! I topple over the image of my brother that's residing in Umma's head — in a way that looks natural and won't make people question anything. It'll be my secret project.

I spent all my time in the days that followed thinking up ways to frame my brother. It wasn't as easy as I'd expected. Every attempt to come up with a plot failed. Like a monastery in Europe carved from rock, my brother stood firm and upright, without a single crevice. He was extremely obnoxious to the last.

Was there any brilliant way I could wreck, at one blow, the image of my brother that Umma held?

It was during the winter break of my first year in middle school, as I was racking my brains practically every day over this issue, that an opportunity presented itself. Isn't it said that the heavens help those who help themselves? Well, it might have come not a little late, but I still feel extremely grateful that the heavens chose, even belatedly, to recognize my efforts.

I believe in fate.

I'm not talking about stuff like falling in love at first sight, of course. Fate is too philosophical, grand, and noble an idea for something so trivial as that. It's like — a revelation from the heavens. It's something ineffable. When you're staring into space and just then a flock of birds flies past, or you're out walking and a falling leaf lands on your head, or it's been raining all day but it stops as you're about to head out — how can you put into words moments like these?

The day I discovered the dog was the most fateful day I'd ever had.

At around 10 p.m., I was cycling home after buying myself some peanut butter cookies at the convenience store when I braked to a halt. I'd just heard a strange noise from inside the deserted park. There was a screeching moan, accompanied by the sound of someone swearing. I got off my bike and crept closer. The mysterious noise was coming from behind the public bathrooms. I squatted behind a bench and stared, holding my breath. I couldn't see anything, as the night was pitch black and the place was far from any streetlamps. After a while, I couldn't hear the strange sounds anymore, either. What, did I hear wrong?

It was right at that moment.

With a sound like grating metal, the moan rose to a climax before exploding with a sudden yelp, like a blowing lightbulb. Silence fell. All the hairs on my body stood up. I swallowed involuntarily. What was that, just now? It was clear something had happened behind the bathrooms. Curiosity, rather than fear, was rising inside me. I wanted to see it. Whatever it was, I wanted to see it for myself...

Just then, something resembling a black plastic bag flew out toward the side of the building. I clapped my hands to my mouth. I'd almost screamed. The thing landed on the ground with a thud and didn't move. Behind it, another shadow came sliding out. Its entrance was definitely different from the one earlier: this time, the thing was walking out by itself. The place was so dark I couldn't see very clearly, but it was a short, skinny man in his forties or fifties. He glanced around, then began to walk over in my direction. Clenching my buttocks, I dropped down flat on the ground. Slowly, the distance between us grew shorter. Damn it — why was he coming this way?

Just then, the man suddenly paused under a streetlight. Had he seen me? My heart felt like it might explode. Thankfully, it didn't seem like he'd caught sight of me, judging by the look on his face. Hey, hang on a minute, that face. It looked familiar — who was it again? Oh yeah — the laundry owner. I always thought he stared at Umma weirdly, and, well, it looks like I was right, he really was a creep. Anyway, what had he been doing down there?

He was staring fixedly at something behind me. Could it be...! It was undeniable. He'd discovered my bike.

I yanked my shoelaces tight, so I could quickly make a run for it if things came to a head. Realizing there was someone else in the park, the man seemed to get nervous and started to chew noisily on a piece of gum he'd hidden beneath his tongue. Then, for whatever reason, he turned back the way he'd come and disappeared behind the bathroom.

After making sure he'd left, I ventured closer to the black bag. Because of how tensely I'd been crouching on the ground, my thighs spasmed with every step.

The thing I'd mistaken for a bag was lying there, motionless, on the dirty sand.

It was a dog the size of a person's forearm.

Its short legs and long body suggested it was a black dachshund. I bent down and examined it closely. Apparently it was still alive; the dog's flat belly was fluttering shallowly. Its paws, which looked like they'd been deliberately declawed, were drenched in sticky blood.

I tried to picture the expressions it must have made as its claws were being torn out. Just imagining it made me feel jumpy and alive. When I thought about how the laundry owner had experienced this feeling all by himself, I grew jealous.

I wanted to feel it, too.

What sort of expression would it make just before it breathed its last? What sort of face would a person make?

I wanted to see my brother make that kind of face.

I thought about him as I grabbed the dog's slender neck and twisted. This must have hurt because the dog whined and writhed its body. It took maybe five seconds. In an instant, its face and body turned into a doll's. How amazing! I'd just experienced an extraordinary moment in which a living thing turned into a mannequin in no more than five seconds.

Right then, a brilliant idea occurred to me.

That's right — my brother becomes the person who murdered the dog. All these years, he's lived life as a good son and model student, but it turns out he's been secretly killing animals in ecstasy. When Umma learns about this, what kind of face will she make? Will she weep, or will she silently shake her head in grave disappointment? Whichever it is, I'll just have to stay by her side and comfort her. Then she'll gaze only at me forever.

I was convinced. Fate! This was fate.

Going to the police was dangerous. The victim's family would be easier to fool than the police.

I'll contact its owner, I decided. I'll make up some reasonable-sounding story about how I stumbled across the dog. Well, that was the truth — to a certain extent, anyway. Then, in gratitude, they'll ask me for my name, at which point I'll tell them my brother's. Several days later, I'll go back to confess that the killer was the informant, me, and to once again reveal my name is Yuchan. It'll be easy to fool them, since my brother and I look so alike that even our relatives get us confused. There'll be less shock value if I tell them it was an accident, so I'll say I did it for fun. Right — it'd be better if I said I hit it deliberately with my bike. Since the words came from the mouth of a teenager, they'll probably believe it. Who knows, they might report it to the police, in which case I — no, my brother — would be called to the police station. How funny would it be if he gets dragged out in front of the whole school!

Newspapers would blare the following headline the next day: "Maths Genius Gong Yuchan, Arrested for Animal Killing!"

I took out my phone and photographed the number written on the collar around its neck. After a couple of rings, there came the voice of a young woman.

"Hello?"

"You haven't lost a dog, by any chance, have you?"

"Sorry… who is this?" The woman's voice quivered. I could sense her wariness.

"I've found the dog, but I think you should come and take a look. The place is — do you know the city library? I'm at the park on the other side of the road."

After a slight hesitation, she replied in a trembling voice that she'd be there, then hung up.

Now that I had to wait, I started to feel hungry. Returning to my bike, I retrieved and opened my bag of peanut butter cookies. I went back to the body and slowly savored the taste of each cookie as it crumbled between my teeth. Crunch, crunch. I ate them while gazing at the dead dog, and they were delicious. The woman arrived by taxi around fifteen minutes later. Judging by the length of time it'd taken her to get here after hanging up the phone, it seemed she lived close by. Our eyes met. She gave a nod of recognition and walked toward me. What — she's old? She looked much older than she'd sounded on the phone. My plan was going to fail. Given how old she was, it was likely she had a kid about my age. That meant she was also likely to feel sympathy toward a boy like me. So many things getting in the way. Like sympathy.

I brought her to the dead body.

It was lying exactly as I'd found it. At first glance, it looked like it could be asleep. Behind me, the woman halted for a very brief second before taking a few slow steps and bending down over it.

"It's time to go home, Bell."

She gently caressed its face, but the dog didn't move. The woman kept saying its name. I fought an urge to yawn. I felt bored and irritated. Couldn't she tell just by looking at it? "Your Bell's dead already," I wanted to tell her, but I decided to keep watching. She was holding the dog tightly in her arms. It was starting to get chilly. Just then, a sharp gust of wind blew past us. I felt my body temperature drop. I wanted to dive immediately under the covers of my bed.

"Are you okay?"

I spoke up because I thought I might freeze to death if I let her go on like this. She whipped around to face me. The nodding woman's face was drenched in tears. Irritation swelled inside me again. What's she bawling for? Does she not care at all that I'm shivering in the cold?

"Thank you, young man, for letting me know," the woman said, wiping her wet cheeks with the palm of her hand.

"It's nothing. Anyone else would have done the same."

What a toe-curling answer.

"How much of a better place the world would be if it was full of brave, good people like you. Oh dear me. I haven't even asked you for your name yet."

With difficulty, I bit back a laugh. She was acting exactly according to my plan.

"I'm Yuchan. Gong Yuchan. I'm in my first year at S Science High School."

Something shifted deep down in the woman's eyes.

My stomach dropped. What if she found it suspicious that I'd been so specific?

"Such a decent-looking boy, and so kindhearted, and good at studying, too. How proud your parents must be. I have a son who's about your age, but he's not exactly normal, you see. It would have been nice if he'd been a little more like you... Oh dear. Look at me, babbling nonsense. It's getting cold, so you should hurry home."

With a wan face, she gathered the limp dog into her arms and walked away. Only then was I able to release the tension in my body. Back home, as I lay in bed, I couldn't get the woman and the dog's corpse out of my mind. At the thought of everything going according to plan, I couldn't fall asleep. It was going perfectly.

She'd taken the bait, more or less. Let's go ahead with the rest of the plan, I thought to myself, and as quickly as possible, while her emotions are still running high. But tomorrow's too soon. The day after tomorrow, then.

I pulled the blanket up to my chin.

Two days later, I visited the woman's home.

To my surprise, she didn't hesitate to give me her address when I contacted her. It's shocking how easily people will trust another person despite knowing nothing about him except his name and the name of his school. The world's full of people who are naive to the point of stupidity.

The address she gave me led to a dirty, run-down fish shop. Of all things, it had to be the thing I hated most.

I loathed everything about fish. Their bulging eyes, their scales, their smell, all of it revolted me. I held my nose while I skulked outside the shop. The woman caught sight of me as she was cleaning fish, and grabbing my hand, she welcomed me inside. I swallowed hard. I fought the urge to break free from her nasty, sticky hands. Ignoring the water she'd poured for me, I got down to business. I admitted to her that I'd discovered her dog on a street corner while out cycling and had deliberately smashed into the animal, thinking it would be fun. She stared at me with a look of disbelief. It was the kind of face I was hoping to see. Wallow in that contempt, indulge yourself.

For a moment, as if lost in thought, the woman did not say anything.

"I understand — you should go on home now. Oh, it said it was going to rain today. Can't be catching a cold. Where did I put that umbrella?"

The woman went back inside the shop and came out with an umbrella, which she handed to me. I was speechless. Some play-acting this was. Was she worried it would rain on someone who'd killed the dog she'd cared for like it was her own child? What a joke. There was no way anyone could be unfazed in a situation like this.

I anticipated success. Any moment now, the woman was going to report the incident, unable to restrain her anger, and all that would remain was for the police to burst in and take my brother away. But two days passed, then four, and nothing happened. Never mind the police; there wasn't even a baby ant lurking at our front door. That idiot woman hadn't called the police after all.

But why? My performance had been perfect!

Blast that woman! Stupid bitch! I should have known the moment I caught that whiff of fish. A dumb, pathetic woman like her would never have been able to appreciate my true objectives. I should have just made sure she'd never find the body. A wave of regret came over me.

At that time, I thought my plan had simply failed.

But the thread of fate turned out to be strong and tough.

On Friday morning, the woman came over to our house. I wasn't interested in how she'd managed to learn my — no, my brother's — address. Once she'd made up her mind, it would have been easy enough to get hold of, since she knew his name and the name of his school. That wasn't the important part.

Why had she come knocking on our door instead of notifying the police?

Okay, that must be why. I'd overestimated her. She must have been even dumber than I'd thought. She'd wanted to inform the boy's parents directly of the truth, and then make them grovel on the spot for her forgiveness.

Yuchan was at his school dormitory, so only Umma and I were at home. Umma was at the front door, talking with the woman. I went upstairs to my room and gazed down at them through the window. I could see their faces relatively clearly but their voices sounded tiny, like a conversation between little people. My mouth went dry. From my desk drawer, I took out a peanut butter cookie and bit down on it. What were they talking about? I cracked open the window, but the voices remained barely audible. Umma was listening to the woman in stony silence, and for a brief second her face contorted. I didn't miss it. My heart was pounding so hard it felt like it might leap out of my chest. At last — success!

Just then, Umma's voice grew strident, so I was able to catch snippets of the conversation.

Umma glared at the woman and accused her son of being the one who killed the dog. She suddenly yelled, demanding proof that the woman's son wasn't the culprit, and I was taken aback by the outburst.

I almost choked on my cookie.

I hadn't expected Umma to say that. Why wasn't she suspicious? Why didn't she suspect in the slightest that my brother could be responsible? Wait a minute! You can't just give up like that and leave, you stupid woman! Furious, I flung my cookie to the floor. I'd never felt like such a fool in my life.

In the end, Umma didn't say anything to Yuchan. Nothing came of it. The woman's visit was wiped clean from her memory as if by an eraser.

Right, another opportunity will present itself. And when it does, I won't make another stupid mistake like this one, I vowed to myself, teeth clenched.

It's something I've noticed for a while, but the sight of girls has no effect on me whatsoever. People often claim one's first love is a giddy, heart-racing experience, but for me, the girl you might call my first love was simply an object I wanted to torment. She was a target to trample on, something I wanted to break — nothing more, nothing less.

We began what you'd call a relationship. It's not like I was in love with her or anything. I only did it because if you didn't have a girlfriend you'd be treated like crap. In our first year of middle school, during the summer vacation, we had our first kiss behind the school building. Were there sparks? Did bells ring in my ears? That's all bullshit. Not only were there zero sparks, but my heart rate stayed the same. It wasn't even as exciting as killing a frog with rocks. There's nothing so boring in this world, I thought, as kissing a woman.

I didn't get it. Dating? Why did people waste their time on something so tedious? The streets were crammed with much more exciting stuff.

It was all boring, simply boring.

I grew tired of my girlfriend. Finding her boring and tedious, I started to hit her. All I did at first was kick her legs. When that grew boring, I began to punch her in the stomach; later, I hit her face. As the days passed, the skin around her eyes turned bluish green. Other people bruised their lips by kissing, but hers were bruised by my fists.

Eventually, Umma was called to the school.

The stupid bitch had gone scurrying to the homeroom teacher to rat on what I'd done to her. I couldn't believe it. Not because she'd betrayed me. For the first time, my mother was coming to visit the school I was enrolled at. And all because of me! This was Umma, who would stop by Yuchan's school like it was her own home.

Umma said she wanted to meet her son's girlfriend in person. The sight of my mother must have scared her because all of a sudden the girl retracted her statement, which meant the enraged teacher merely shouted abuse at the girl and the incident came to a very bland end. I'd hoped for something more dramatic.

When we got home that night, Umma sat me down on the sofa and said quietly, "Be honest with me. What's your relationship with that girl?"

She was being quite serious, but I was deeply moved. For the first time in my life, she was showing me an excessive amount of interest.

"I didn't realize, but I think she secretly liked me."

"So you're telling me that everything she said was a lie that she told to get your attention?"

I nodded. She looked awkward for a moment, and then muttered, "Just as I expected."

"I'm okay. She had the hardest time of it, I think."

Umma stared at me with surprise on her face. I knew what that meant. Clearly, it was a look of compassion. She was feeling pity for her poor son.

But she doesn't know yet.

That all I need is Umma herself. What I desire is not Umma's love, but simply her attention. I wasn't interested in love or anything like that.

The next day, Dong-gyu was full of admiration when I told him about the incident the previous week.

"That's so fucking cool!"

He asked me what it'd felt like to kill a dog, so I described it for him in detail—as scarily and gruesomely as possible. His face grew strangely contorted. Whenever I see a face like that, I'm so tickled it makes me want to puke. Stupid morons, sticking their noses into stuff they can't even handle. The classroom is swarming with them. At lunchtime, everyone who'd heard the rumors clustered around me and pelted me with questions. It was irritating, but I was prepared to repeat the story one more time. But abruptly, seemingly carried away with excitement, Dong-gyu cut in and started describing it even more brutally than before. How dare he swoop in and snatch away my joy? Should I teach him a lesson?

"That's so sick!" someone said. "So when are you going to do it again?"

The question came as a blow. It was a problem I hadn't considered before. Honestly, I hadn't been intending to make it a one-time thing, either. Feel a pleasure like that only once? Only idiots make that kind of mistake.

"Tomorrow at midnight, in the empty lot next to Saehan Car Park."

In unison they cried, "Wow," and cheered.

I was actually a little surprised. Who'd have thought so many of them would feel as I did? In that light, grown-ups are seriously pathetic. Even now, they believe that teenagers are pure of heart. They think we don't know anything. They think we never feel pain, that we don't know about discrimination or the desire to kill, or anything else — even though we, like them, know everything there is to know. We know what it's like to receive pain and to give it, too. Grown-ups need to realize that if they look down their noses at us, they're going to pay for it. Anyway, do I carry out the work with these morons or not?

"If you want to do this with me, it can't be for free. Starting tomorrow, each of us should take turns bringing a dog. It doesn't matter how many, or what size. Since we're just starting, though, smaller ones might be better."

I hated to make stuff complicated, so I suggested going by the order of class number. The others agreed without protest. Right then, someone piped up.

"But how do we find our targets?"

I felt irritated. Losers like him always needed stuff explained to them. They wouldn't recognize art even if it hit them in the eye.

"It's up to you," I forced out.

Just then the bell rang, and everyone scattered to their seats. Resting my chin on my hand, I mulled things over. Maybe this was for the best. It'd be easier to collect targets as a group than do it on my own. Dong-gyu turned around and gave me a wink. I smiled inwardly. Just don't overdo it tomorrow, fool.

The next day, at midnight.

I arrived first at the vacant lot and waited for the others to get there. A new person showed up every three minutes, and about fifteen minutes later it seemed nearly everyone had arrived. There were six of us in total, including me. I couldn't see a few faces from yesterday, but it was still a pretty solid turnout. Those cowards would only slow us down, anyway. They'd probably snivel in fear. For some reason, though, everyone had come empty-handed.

"Number Three, wasn't it your turn?" I asked a pudgy boy, the top of whose head barely reached my upper chest.

"I did find one, actually," he hedged, in a thin, mosquito's voice, "but I didn't think I could bring it here all by myself."

"Where?"

"In front of the recycling center. It's not far from here."

"If it's not there, you're getting expelled from the group. You already knew that, right?"

Number Three hung his head and nodded weakly.

Just as he'd described, there was a yellowish mutt in front of the recycling center. It was slightly larger than a Jindo dog, and clearly a mongrel of some kind. A tether was hanging around its thick neck. Things were going frustratingly badly. It was only day one, and we had to deal with this stupid business of cutting a tether. Drawing closer, I inspected the material. At least it was made out of rope, which could be sliced through with a knife, rather than metal.

The dog appeared to be as stupid as it looked. Rather than bark at us, it gently wagged its tail. Abruptly, Number Eight reached out a hand and said, "Come here, doggy." So unnecessary. Still wagging its tail, the dog trotted over to us. "Oh, what a clever boy," Eight said admiringly. "Seems like a waste to kill it." Pathetic. Why can't they tell that the more obedient it is, the more thrilling it is to kill it? Do they even realize what an important and artistic undertaking this is? They're idiots who don't know what it means to be sincere in all your efforts.

I took a box cutter from my bag and sawed at the tether. The mutt kept licking my face so it took a while. Dragging the dog with us, we headed to the lot. Like earlier, no one else was there. It was pretty much the perfect spot for our work. Anyway, what masterpiece shall we produce today? Since we were doing this for the first time as a group, we decided to choose the method of participation by majority rule. How about burying it alive, was the very first suggestion. That's too boring, I said, so how about we pummel it first to our hearts' content and then bury it afterward when it's barely breathing. Everyone agreed.

Each of us picked up a discarded beam of wood. The dog, whose tether was being held by Number Eight, had tucked its tail between its quivering legs. It seemed to have finally grasped the situation. For an instant, my eyes met the dog's, and my heart froze over.

It was beautiful.

The sight of it trembling in fear, aware of its impending death — how beautiful it was!

All living things are at their most beautiful just before they die. The dog looked a bit stupid because of the way it kept yapping, but apart from that, everything was perfect.

I let Dong-gyu have the first go. I meant it as a thoughtful gesture between close friends. But not realizing what a great honor it was, he just stood there, gulping, clutching his wooden beam. Small wonder: if you're stupid, you don't even know how to use the opportunities you're given.

PETTY LIES

I had no choice but to set an example. With a spin of my wrist, I gently swung my beam. Just then the target shifted position, and so, despite aiming for the head, I ended up hitting it on the front legs. A cheery "Yap!" burst from the target's mouth. One of its legs must have broken, because it kept lowering its upper body as it limped around, making it look like it was bowing. It was hilarious. I was beside myself with laughter.

Number Three followed with a smack to the rump. Number Sixteen struck the hind legs, Twenty-Two the lower back, while Thirty-Five — Dong-gyu — rather unimaginatively hit the front legs, like I had, and Number Eight, who was still holding on to the tether, thumped its chest. Like a top, the target spun round and round before collapsing to the ground.

I felt purged inside. It felt like I'd just watched an episode of a comedy show.

It had taken maybe about ten minutes. We were done with the work sooner than I'd anticipated.

Calmly, I gazed around at each of their faces. They looked deathly pale. Their faces seemed to show a mixture of emotions — contempt, fear, a hint of pleasure, relief it was over. Most plainly visible was fear. It had scared them that much? The more I got to know them, the more I realized how pathetic and surprising they were.

"If anyone wants to quit, it's better to say so now."

Looking dazed, the five of them turned together to stare at me. All five pairs of eyes seemed to be asking, Who exactly are you? Are you saying you're not frightened, even after that?

That was the truth. I wasn't frightened at all. They'd never known anything truly scary. What's really scary isn't stuff like that buried dog over there. Real terror is my mother's and brother's eyes ignoring me. It's when I think I've become a transparent bubble. That crap makes me feel so worthless I want to die. There's nothing more scary in the world than becoming worthless.

"I'm not interested in forcing anyone to do it. It's easier on my own, anyway."

I left them blinking dumbly and went home. The clock read a little past 1 a.m. when I got back. As I was getting into bed, a flurry of text messages arrived.

All five said they would join the group.

Increasingly, our methods escalated in intensity.

We tried placing our targets inside a fridge to time how long they lasted, and we also drove nails into their feet like Jesus Christ. One thing I noticed while doing this work was that dogs had a remarkably tenacious will to live. It drove Dong-gyu and a few others up the wall, but for me it came as a fresh surprise — that even such insignificant creatures would flail around in order to live.

What was it for, exactly, that they thrashed and struggled so they wouldn't die? For what reason did they have to live?

It was ugly. Ugly and vulgar.

Well, if they didn't even have this vulgar survival instinct, I guess it wouldn't be very fun.

If it went away, things would get awkward. It's my only pleasure in life.

Something else I noticed was how the police took no action, even when dogs with owners were evidently being killed outdoors. All they did was hang up a banner outside the police station warning people about a dog killer. It shocked me. Rather than astonishment, I felt respect. In this country, animal killings seemed to be nothing more than a trivial matter, beyond what I had expected. How lucky I am to have been born in a country like this!

Somehow, Umma seemed to realize something was going on. Out of the blue, she asked me if I wouldn't be interested in getting some private tutoring. She already knew I'd hate it, yet she kept repeating herself, insistent.

"Remember Huijeong, my friend from college? Her daughter managed to get into S University after being tutored by this teacher. She wasn't even among the top ten students in her class, originally. So you can do it, too. What do you say?"

Umma knows. About the kind of stuff my friends and I are getting up to. And she's clearly pretending not to know, pretending it's for the sake of my grades. How did she find out? It wouldn't have been obvious. And if she knows about it, why isn't she angry with me? Does she think even that is a waste of her time?

"Okay. I'll do as you say, Umma."

At my reply, I saw her face gentle for the very first time. I was hoping she would get angry, but this wasn't so bad, either.

Anyway, a private tutor. I'm looking forward to seeing what kind of loser he is.

"So you're Yujae. I'm Kim Minhyeok, and I'll be teaching you from now on."

He looked like someone with an illness. This man with his sloping eyebrows and a face so chalky white it looked like it'd been powdered was saying that he hoped we would get along. I was about to ignore him but Umma was watching, so I forced myself to say I was glad to meet him. The sickly-looking man sat me down and spent thirty minutes reeling off a bunch of nonsense.

"Your mother tells me you used to get good grades in the past. I know it's a turbulent time for you right now. For a while when I was your age, I went through something similar, too. I'd try to study but I'd lose focus, and my mind would start wandering. I'd grow interested in the opposite sex, or I'd start thinking about the games at the arcade. But it's during times like these that you've got to get a grip on yourself. If you manage to get through this now, life will get a lot easier later."

The opposite sex? The arcade? I almost burst out laughing.

"Childish stuff like that might apply to you," I wanted to shout in his face, "but the work I do is so much greater than that. It's the sort of thing you people wouldn't dare to imitate."

He and Umma had got it all wrong, and by a huge margin. I wasn't studying for reasons that were yawn-inducingly simple.

It had nothing to do with turbulent times, or whatever. Stuff like that only applied to wimps.

So, what's the reason?

There isn't one.

I don't study because I simply don't want to.

If I had to give a more concrete reason, I'd say it's because I want my mother's attention. It's because I want to get under her skin at the same time. Because I want to see her suffer and be anxious because of me. So she'll have no choice but to be concerned about me, so that I won't pop like a bubble. So that, like a needle stabbing at her finger, I can carve, in her mind, the fact of my existence, the fact that I'm not a bubble but a whole person.

The man said he'd come over three times a week. As many as three times. Umma must have asked him to keep an eye on me. As a result, the time I could spend doing the work shrank to four days.

Well, whatever. I'll just have to put the weekend and the remaining two days to good use.

The way I see it, there's nothing easier than deceiving other people.

As long as you don't talk back, and faithfully do as you're told, you become a good son and a model student. To my tutor, I was a good student who met those conditions. I never put off doing my homework, and I did what he asked me to do without grumbling, and completed difficult assignments with ease. I'd found those problems incredibly easy to solve, but the tutor seemed to think I'd worked hard to prepare for my tutorials and review the material. I didn't bother to correct him. It wasn't doing me any disservice, after all.

On the contrary, I gained so much more from it. He didn't hold back in his praise for me to my mother, which must have pleased her, because her attitude toward me began to change. Before long I became a good son. When I brought friends home, she no longer considered them a nuisance but treated them kindly, even bringing us peeled apple slices, which she'd rarely offered even to me. At some point I introduced Dong-gyu, explaining that he was the class monitor, and with a bright smile she told him he could sleep over.

I'd never seen her smile at me like that.

For a second my stomach twisted. What was it about me that my mother hated so much? Was it the fact I wasn't a class monitor? But that didn't make sense. My brother hadn't been one, either.

Then was it because I resembled my dad's side of the family? Because I was just another son and not a daughter?

Right, it could only be for the following reason:

I wasn't Yuchan. I wasn't my dratted older brother.

That's what my mother hated most about me.

But what if he were to disappear?

No doubt, that position would become mine alone. Then Umma would gaze only at me.

It made my whole body tingle just to imagine it.

PETTY LIES

. . .

Evading the watchful eyes of my mother and tutor, I'd managed to carry out the work about ten times.

By that point, the desire to brag about it to someone was greater than the pleasure of killing dogs in secret. I needed a person who'd recognize and appreciate my artistic endeavors. I puzzled over whom that could be.

The teachers at my school? Those dumb idiots wouldn't understand it even if it killed them. They justify any acts of violence they commit, but they'll belittle ours as pathetic acts of rebelliousness.

My classmates? No, they're babies. I want recognition from someone more mature.

Then what about my tutor? He's too close to my mother. And he doesn't seem intelligent enough to understand my world. He'll just rattle off another boring sermon. I'd rather post stuff on the internet, even with its horde of idiots.

It was disheartening. I was feeling disappointed that there wasn't a single person who would understand me.

Right then, she appeared. My new tutor.

Yoon Mira. Twenty-five years old. She was a self-possessed and refined-looking young woman, but there seemed to be a darkness somewhere inside her. People say like recognizes like. I could read the rage in her eyes. I had no idea what she was angry about, but it was obvious in any case that she'd suffered a great deal of misfortune. I was excited. I hadn't felt this excited in a while.

Who knows — this woman might be able to understand my artistic pursuits.

Had she felt the same things that I had?

The new tutor seemed to take a keen interest in me. She asked me loads of questions, like the date of my birth, my favorite subjects, novels that had left the greatest impression on me, and so on. It was tedious, but strangely enough I didn't mind it so much. Now, that was startling. I was surprised at myself for answering each of her questions so patiently.

"Didn't that hurt?" she once asked, pointing at the scar on my left ear.

For a second I felt nauseated, as if from motion sickness, and my heart was pounding. Nobody had ever asked me this question before. Not even my mother.

I'd always wanted to know why Umma had given birth to me. My curiosity was so great that I felt like grabbing any random person off the street to ask them this question. In Yuchan, my mother had a perfect son. She'd often say — seemingly out of habit — that having one son was enough. She said stuff like that whenever I was around as if she intended for me to hear it. No matter whether I wanted to or not, I listened to her say those words over and over again. It would've been better if I'd been born deaf.

So I'd stabbed my ear with a fork. I was seven years old.

Umma frowned but didn't say anything. She didn't ask me why I'd hurt myself or whether I was in pain. She stared at me with a look that seemed to say: wipe away that dirty blood at once. I found the ointment and put it on by myself. Oddly, it didn't hurt at all. Some other part of me was hurting. In fact, I was disappointed to hear everything around me so clearly. Would my mother have worried about me if I'd used a chopstick to stab myself more deeply? I felt regret.

I just wanted to hear it. I wanted to hear my mother speak to me tenderly, in a voice full of concern, the way other mothers spoke to their children. But it was my tutor — whom I'd known for barely a week — who was using this voice as she questioned me.

"It's even left a scar. How did it happen?"

She was looking at my ear sorrowfully. I wanted to reward her for her concern. How do I make this more interesting? Suddenly, that loser came to mind.

"My brother stabbed me. With a fork."

"Your brother?" she repeated, sounding shocked, just as I'd expected her to.

"Yes."

"Why did he do it?"

"It happens all the time. Whenever he's in a bad mood, he takes it out on me, like this."

"Oh...I see."

What? That was weird.

Usually, if someone told you a boy stabbed his younger brother with a fork, weren't you supposed to react with suspicion or dismay?

But the tutor began explaining a formula as if nothing had

happened. Really, you didn't find that shocking? I was disappointed. She'd spoiled the party and ended things on a boring note. I'd been hoping for a more forceful reaction. My feeling of goodwill toward her plummeted sharply to the ground.

It wasn't long before it rose again, though. One day, she brought with her a novel that she recommended I read. It was Dostoyevsky's *The Brothers Karamazov*.

"You'll like it. When you're done with this, I'll get you another one."

Subsequently, she lent me Hermann Hesse's *Demian*, Emily Brontë's *Wuthering Heights*, and Albert Camus's *The Stranger*. We'd discuss the books during the breaks. Sometimes, after telling me to read, she'd quietly leave the room to explore the house. I didn't bother asking her why. It was obvious she was doing it out of consideration for me. She knew how not to irritate people, it seemed. She was polite to a point, and also indifferent to a point. She wasn't apathetic like my mother, and she didn't prattle on noisily like my previous tutor. It was the first time, I felt, that I'd met a proper adult.

As the time I spent reading increased, the time I'd set aside for that other work naturally dwindled. One day at school, the five of them, including Dong-gyu, protested. They surrounded me in the corridor and demanded to know the reason why.

"I've grown weary of it," I replied.

Inwardly, I marveled. Grow weary. Such a tasteful expression, every time. Devoting yourself to only one activity made you look boring and ignorant.

All five of them stared at me, stunned, their mouths hanging open. How would babies like you understand, anyway? Have a go at it without me. Waving goodbye, I entered the classroom.

If there was one thing about the tutor that rubbed me the wrong way, it was the fact that she seemed interested in my brother as well.

She asked me what my relationship with him was like, but she also wanted to know about his health, if he had any allergies or took any special medication. I laughed inwardly. I resisted the urge to say: "How great would it be if he had anything like that?"

But my brother was excessively healthy. At most, he'd catch a cold. Had he been born under a lucky star? It annoyed me. I might have some kind of fatal illness; meanwhile, he was as hearty as ever. Fortunately, the thought that I might have contracted a fatal illness was a mistake.

I found out purely by chance that I might have a disease.

After returning home from school, I was about to enter the bathroom when my throat began to sting terribly. A wave of pain overcame me like I'd swallowed a whole razor. Holding a hand to my mouth, I coughed, almost spasming. I felt a warm fluid splatter on my palm. At first, I assumed it was just saliva. But as soon as I grabbed the faucet to wash my hands, I realized it wasn't.

Bright red blood.

It was definitely blood.

Not dark red but vivid, scarlet blood.

What is this? I'd coughed, but then blood had come out.

My mind went white. I wasn't sure what to do, so I just left the bathroom and went to my room. I turned on the computer and typed "coughing up blood symptom" into an online search window. Tuberculosis, fungal infection, bronchiectasis. There were only unfamiliar words on the screen. One word stood out, at least a little familiar to my eyes: tuberculosis. Right, I'd heard that you cough up blood if you catch tuberculosis. Did this mean I was going to die?

I'm going to die. I'm dying. I'm dying, I'm dying!

No, there might be a way. But I didn't want to go to the hospital. I hated the thought of a doctor looking at me pityingly even more than the prospect of dying. For some reason, doctors look pathetic and mournful to me.

I needed some other person.

I needed someone other than a doctor, who would feel sorry for me. Someone who'd be able to help me.

I went immediately to my brother's room. I don't know why. At the time I couldn't think of any other place. It was a Saturday, so he was at home. I knocked on the door and opened it. A Seo Taiji song was drifting from the speakers. Yuchan was lying on his bed, listening to music. His eyes were closed and he didn't move a muscle, so I couldn't tell whether he was aware I'd come in.

"Get up."

He opened his eyes a crack, saw me, then closed them again.

"What is it?"

I struggled to hold back the rage swelling inside me. Get up, I said! Your brother is here! Can't you see me?

"There's something wrong with my body."

"In what way?"

He was looking at me now. I guess he felt concerned.

"I coughed up blood," I said, trying to sound as pitiful as possible.

Eyes widening, he partially raised himself and turned off the music.

"Describe to me what happened."

"Just a second ago I was coughing, and then blood came out. I thought it was saliva at first and was about to wash my hand, but it was covered in red liquid."

"Are you sure?"

"About what?"

"That it was really blood?"

"You think I wouldn't be able to tell the difference?"

"Could it have come from your palm somewhere? You might have hurt yourself without realizing it."

"I've checked, but I'm not hurt anywhere."

"Let's have a look."

I went to him and showed him my palm.

"Does Umma know about this?"

I shook my head. Then, was he the first person I talked to? he wanted to know. I nodded. Why? he asked. Why? Well, actually, why had I come running to his room? Had I been hoping he would do something for me? That loser? Was my head affected somehow?

Maybe I was hoping he would worry about me. Or I'd wanted to check if I really was a bubble to him or not.

I was just standing there, so he said he understood, now could I go back to my room for a second. I did as I was told. I went inside my room and sank down on my bed. My heart was racing uncontrollably. I started chewing my thumbnail, something I'd never done before in my life. It didn't make me feel any calmer, so I pulled my blanket over my head and let out a hysterical scream like an insane person. Me, I'm going to die? But I'm not a fool. Only fools died like this. Dying while coughing up blood! It made no sense, I couldn't die such a miserable death.

Just then, my brother came in through the door. I snatched the blanket away from my face, not wanting to look stupid. He was gazing at me sympathetically. It was the first time that he'd looked at me like that. Quick, tell me you feel sorry for me! "My poor baby brother" — say it, quick!

Perching on a chair, he fixed his eyes on me and asked, "Did you cough a lot recently?"

Cough? Now that I thought about it, I might have. I nodded.

"Tell me if there's pain anywhere else. Like if you have a headache, or feel pain around the waist."

"I don't feel anything."

"Are you sure?"

"Yeah."

His voice relaxed a little.

"As far as I can tell, you seem to have a slight cut on the inside of your throat. That happens sometimes, apparently. For it to be tuberculosis, there has to be noticeable weight loss, but since that's not the case, it can't be that."

I wasn't going to die? Overwhelmed with happiness, I almost skipped for joy.

There was no way I could have died such a vulgar death. Ha ha ha — I wasn't going to die. I knew I wasn't like those fools.

The matter was now resolved, but my brother still did not leave. In a sincere tone of voice, he went on:

"I've been thinking about this, and if I don't bring it up now I think I'll regret it."

"What do you mean, regret?"

What was he going on about? At a moment like this, no less.

"Late last Sunday night, out there in the empty lot — it was you and your friends, wasn't it, mistreating a dog? I saw it by accident, on my way back from the convenience store. I know that probably wasn't the first time you did it, either. Willingly or not, I want you to reflect on yourself and repent of your actions. And promise me you won't do it anymore. Umma doesn't know about it yet. You wouldn't want her to find out, would you?"

What kind of response was this?

You have no idea how worried sick I was, thinking I might lose you, Yujae; I'm so relieved you're not going to die. Isn't that what's normally supposed to come out? I wasn't even asking for tears. But when your only baby brother has come back from the dead, shouldn't you look happy about it, at least?

Like hell he's my brother. Is he even qualified to be my hyung? A loser like him — who's off worrying about other people when his baby brother is dying — doesn't deserve to be called a hyung. Why feel sorry for people who are sniveling just because a mongrel dog died, anyway? And it's not like I've ever given him permission to be my hyung, either.

Why does everyone behave like I don't exist in their eyes? Just how did he react when I told him I'd coughed up blood, when I said it was likely I had a fatal illness? What did he say to me without changing expression? Go back to your room. And what, now? Repent? Fuck repentance, feed it to the dogs. What did I ever do to them? What's so great about that loser? A pathetic coward like him. Why does Umma like that loser son of hers so much?

Why is it him, and not me, who makes her smile?

I am the only good son to my mother. Only I, and not that nasty, depraved loser, can live entirely for her sake. It's enough to have just one son like me by her side.

I'll crush you under my feet. Hyung.

"Okay. I won't do it again," I replied, biting down hard on my lip.

I was well acquainted with his weaknesses.

Acrophobia. The condition where if you go somewhere high

up, you get the shakes, like those dogs I work on. Once, when I was eight and he was twelve, we both got on a glass elevator inside a building and to my shock he went insane. At first, I thought he was putting on an act. A performance to get our mother's attention. But when I saw tears and snot dribbling down his face, I realized he wasn't acting. If I can make good use of this weakness, I might be able to pop him.

What a vision. He falls from a great height and explodes with a bang. Like a water-filled balloon.

What would be a good location?

Places like building rooftops are out of the question, since they're danger zones and they'll all be locked up. Somewhere inconspicuous, a place where no one would be very shocked if someone fell down. And most of all, somewhere without CCTV.

Just then, the perfect spot flashed through my mind like an electric spark.

That's it — the pedestrian overpass in front of the elementary school was ideal. But who was going to lure him there?

I had run into an unexpected problem. He'd obviously grow suspicious if I asked him to go. And he was never going to listen to me, anyway. Damn it, how was I supposed to lure him? As far as I was aware, he was a dork who'd never gone out with a girl. I might as well get a girl to do it...

It was about half an hour later that she popped into my head. The stalker who pursued me almost every day.

Shall I say hello to her tomorrow after school?

. . .

There she is!

She's following me again today. I don't know her name. I don't recognize her middle school uniform, either. All I know is that she's this pathetic kid who stalks me pretty much every day. Her face looks like — what's her name, the actress who frequently shows up in adverts. The one with the surname Song, I think. Anyway, she looks like her. In short, she's the cute type. I don't really know what's considered cute, but since people say that actress is cute, that girl's face becomes cute, too, automatically.

I used to feel something like pity for her, once. How boring must her life be to go around stalking someone? Deep down, does she want to die, too? Does she want me to kill her? was my thought.

"Hey."

Bringing my bike to a standstill, I turned around and called her over. It must have flustered her because she dropped her gaze and pretended to be doing something else.

"I'm talking to you, Yellow Scarf. I know you've been following me."

She glanced around, eyes darting here and there, before timidly making her way toward me.

"Since when did you know about me?"

"From the start."

"How?"

"Who wouldn't when you're wearing a scarf like that? Next time, maybe wear a color that's less striking."

She kept fingering her scarf, in apparent embarrassment.

"What's your name?"

"Yi Songhui…"

"Yi Songhui, you're going to have to help me."

"Me? How?"

Her face suddenly grew animated at the prospect. How pathetic. Do you even know what it is I'm asking you to do?

"You just have to do as I tell you."

I explained the plan I'd worked out earlier last night before going to sleep.

She feigns an interest in my brother and hands him a love letter. → When he starts to respond, the two of them start seeing each other in earnest. → She says she wants to choose the location for their date. → She suggests the café on the other side of the overpass. → While crossing the overpass, she pretends to look down, then pushes him from behind. → He falls onto the traffic-laden asphalt road.

The probability of success was 100 percent. Even I thought it was a breathtaking plan.

"But would I be able to do something like that…?"

I'd been expecting that. It meant she wanted something in return. Unpleasant bitch.

As a condition of our agreement, I'd do "it" for her, I said, and she tilted her head to one side. What's that? she asked. What

I mean is this, I said, and pointed back and forth between our lips. When she finally realized what I meant, she flushed bright red. If I pressed my finger down, she might explode.

Evidently, she'd wanted to kiss me. A girl in middle school, admitting to stuff like that. Had she routinely fantasized about doing that sort of thing with me? A chill ran down my spine.

"You know, I have a request of my own."

She didn't seem to have grasped that only I could make requests. Poor thing. I might as well have a listen.

"What is it?"

"I want you to give me a sense of certainty."

"Certainty?"

"Yes."

This part I hadn't anticipated. It was my mistake for having underestimated her.

"What do I have to do, to give you certainty?"

Again, her face quickly turned red.

This was outrageous. She'd been acting all shy and modest, and now she wanted this from me? "Just forget the whole thing," I wanted to tell her, but not having her take part in the plan would make things awkward. I bent forward slightly and brought my face closer to hers. I brushed my lips against her cheek, which was as cold as a mannequin. For a moment I felt her body stiffen like a rod. It inspired nothing in me.

"Done?" I asked, lifting my head. I felt soiled, as if I'd just touched something I shouldn't have.

PETTY LIES

It was already over, but she didn't raise her head. And then, as if struck by the thought of what had just happened, she gave a bashful smile. What an idiot. Girls are all so stupid. If they like someone, they'll believe everything he says. Don't they know you can't trust what a man tells you? Well, it's worked out well for me, but still.

"Just keep your promise."

She nodded eagerly, and I stepped on the pedal, leaving her standing there by herself.

For several weeks, I kept a close watch on my brother. Nothing much changed during that first week. But later I began to notice slight differences in his behavior. He kept fidgeting with his phone as if he was waiting for a message, and more than once, I caught him swiftly tucking something under his notes as Umma entered his room without knocking. The way he looked at me changed, too. Before, he'd have swept past me like I was a ghost, but now he'd look on, leaking smiles like a flat tire. That was a good sign. Though I didn't like the way he kept laughing while looking at me. Not long now, before they play Romeo and Juliet.

December 11

I took Yellow Scarf to an alley and instructed her to go on the date the next day. Giving no reply, she only stared at the ground. When I asked her if she'd heard me, she finally nodded, and then mumbled in a small voice, "Um, can we not do this anymore? I don't think I can do it."

"You're telling me this now? Did you forget our promise?"

"No."

"Then, shut your mouth."

"But it's your own hyung. Why are you trying to kill him?"

"That's none of your business. Just do as I tell you."

"I don't want to. I'm so scared, I can't do it."

"All right, I'll tell you why I want to kill my brother. It's because of Umma. Her attention is completely focused on him, and that drives me crazy. Being the younger sibling is like crap. So, he has to disappear. That way, Umma will pay attention to me. Now do you get it?"

"No, I don't understand. If you want to kill him that much, do it yourself. But you're too scared to do it, too, that's why, right?"

Sparks exploded before my eyes.

They just won't listen to you if you talk to them nicely. I was disappointed. I hadn't intended to resort to crude methods. With all the strength I had, I grabbed her by the throat and spoke to her threateningly.

"If you don't do it, just remember you're going to die instead. I'm not joking. You've been following me around, so you know what I've been up to in the empty lot. Do you or don't you?"

Yellow Scarf nodded with difficulty. I shoved her against the wall, hard enough to dislocate a shoulder, then released her.

"Tomorrow, at 9 p.m. It'd be best if you don't have second thoughts. Because I'll be watching."

Yellow Scarf wheezed and coughed, struggling for breath, then finally vomited. A disgusting smell rose in the air. She really was a pathetic bitch, from start to finish. I quickly headed home before the smell could get on my clothes. As I closed the front door behind me, my brother, in a rare move, spoke to me first.

"You wouldn't have forgotten the promise you made to me last time?"

But of course. "Don't worry," I lied, forcing a smile. "I really won't do it again."

"Good choice." He tousled my hair, making a mess of it. Then he smirked in my direction. Yeah, smile all you want. Because even if you wanted to, you won't be able to after tomorrow.

I went to my room and immediately messaged Dong-gyu. **Tomorrow, at 8 p.m.** I'd already made sure our stories matched. At around 8 p.m., he goes to the movies with another friend, who'll act as my stand-in. They decide to see an action movie, a genre we like. When it ends, they hang around until midnight at the arcade inside the theater before heading home. The next day, I receive the movie ticket in exchange for my *game console. And like that, I obtain an alibi for 9 p.m. tomorrow.*

It doesn't look like Dong-gyu's realized just yet what it is I'm trying to achieve at the cost of my beloved console. When he finds out what I'm doing is on a different scale from them — since the most they can do is kill dogs — what kind of face will he make? He'd be so proud to have a friend by his side who's capable of killing a person.

My phone beeped.

Okay! We exchange goods in the classroom on Monday!

Dong-gyu won't ever find out, not until I tell him personally. Poor bastard. Shall I just make sure he never does find out?

I turned my phone off.

December 12
8:30 p.m.

Yellow Scarf rang me to say she was on her way to meet my brother. Arriving early at the café on the other side of the street, I took a seat by the window with the best view of the overpass. I was emphatic about the fact that I'd be watching her. "If I don't see you at the agreed time, I won't be leaving you alone," I warned her once more. Then I added, "The same *goes even if he doesn't show up."* In a trembling voice, she told me not to worry and hung up.

My heart was beating so loudly I could hear it.

I felt excited. This was more exciting than the secret nighttime work. I would have liked to step in and do everything myself—that went without saying—but as far as intensity and the fun of it went, being a spectator wasn't half bad, either.

A heavily freckled employee came up to me and, to my annoyance, asked for my order. I said I just wanted an orange juice. When I checked my phone, it was already 8:50 p.m. I turned my head and stared out the window. Someone had just arrived on the other side of the road. Yellow Scarf. It was Yi Songhui. I laughed. She clearly hadn't wanted to die.

Five minutes went by before my brother finally made his appearance. The two of them exchanged a few words and then began to climb the overpass. I was astonished. I began to wonder if he was the same boy I knew. He was bounding up the stairs with so much vigor that it was a shame only I was there to see it. It was then that I understood how mighty the power of woman could be.

Oh yeah, that's right! Why don't I record this on my phone, so that I can brag about it to Dong-gyu later?

I searched for the camera app on my phone and hit the record button. It was too bad their faces came out the size of beans on the screen. At last, the two reached the halfway point of the overpass. Any moment now, he would explode. Pop!

They stuck close to the railing. Now's the moment! Come on, push! Push! I screamed silently. Just then, the employee returned with the orange juice, so I almost missed this most magnificent moment. Taking a second to calm my rattled nerves, I quickly turned my eyes back to the overpass. They were still standing there, side by side. What could they be doing? I was so exasperated that my heart felt like bursting. I wanted to run down there at once and push him myself.

But then the most monstrous thing happened.

Yellow Scarf did not push him. She seemed to say something instead, and then turned away to walk toward the stairs. My brother followed, stumbling.

Had she told him? That I'd made her do everything? That idiot who goes around stalking people — surely not?

My breathing grew so fast I found it hard to inhale and exhale.

Just then, the girl suddenly crouched in front of the stairway, as if her shoelaces had come undone. My brother had to move past and start descending the steps before her. It was right at that moment. Yellow Scarf leapt up and pushed at his back with both hands. Slowly at first, then all at once, his body rolled down the steps like a wheel. Pop! it wasn't. Yellow Scarf stood still, observing. But wait, the angle of her head...?

For a second my heart stopped beating.

The girl was staring at me, not my brother. I couldn't see her face clearly, but I knew. That stupid bitch, gazing down in my direction, was sneering at me right now.

I jumped to my feet. I could feel other people's eyes on me, but I couldn't stand it.

It was humiliating.

No doubt she'd been planning to do this all along. To screw me over, that cunning bitch had pushed him at the top of the steps instead of the overpass!

December 16

Following on from last year's failure, I'd failed once again.

One failure after another, like an idiot. It was degrading.

But the situation wasn't entirely bad. If you looked at it another way, it was half a success.

A coma.

My brother lay unconscious in a hospital room. The body was there, but not the mind. Therefore, his lack of consciousness was no different from half of him exploding — though, of course, one half wasn't enough. On the contrary, it had the opposite effect. Umma began to shower my brother with more tenderness than ever before. This wasn't it. This wasn't what I wanted. I won't be satisfied until Umma focuses her attention solely on me.

Now it's a question of when to pop the remaining half. Well, I can think about that in my own time; first, how do I take care of that bitch?

I did consider forgiving her at first, in spite of her occasional rudeness, since the stalker bitch had managed to complete half the task. But the fact that I'd been made a fool of wasn't something I could tolerate. I went over to her school — which I'd staked out in advance, knowing something like this might happen — and waited outside the main gates. I caught sight of her as she passed through. Yellow Scarf saw me at the same time and, blanching, began to run in the opposite direction. She must have forgotten that I had a bicycle. To think I'd been outwitted by this idiot. It was so maddening I couldn't stand it. I chased her at full speed, and as she fled into a car park next to a church, I seized her by the hair.

"Please don't kill me!" the girl begged, squealing like a stuck pig.

"I'm pretty sure I told you to do as I said."

"I pushed him at the overpass like you wanted me to! Wasn't that enough?"

"Get your facts straight. I never said to push him down the stairs, I told you to push him from the top of the overpass."

I yanked her hair hard enough to snap the strands.

"That hurts, let go of me! You're just a coward with an inferiority complex!"

For a second, I couldn't believe my ears.

"What did you say?"

"You want me to say it again since you didn't hear me the first time? I said you're a coward! You're scared, aren't you, that you'll always come second to your hyung? You seem to think that if he's gone, you'll have your umma's love all to yourself, but get real! All that love might go to your dead brother, but it definitely won't go to you. And you didn't realize any of this — are you an idiot? I feel pathetic for ever having liked you!"

I was stunned. Had this stupid bitch just called me a coward and an idiot?

Just then, the girl struggled so wildly that a button popped off one of my sleeves. In that same instant, my patience snapped. I got off my bike, and with all the force I could muster I kicked the girl's flat stomach. Yellow Scarf retched in pain, but I didn't stop. I'd only kicked her a few times when, like an egg that had been placed vertically, she toppled over.

"Hey, get up. I know you're awake."

I nudged her with my foot a couple of times, but she didn't even twitch. She was lying face down in the same pose that dogs assumed just before they died. Surely she hadn't died? Not this easily? I grabbed her by the shoulder and shook her, hard. There was no response. I brought my hand to her nose. I couldn't feel any air going in and out. Wait, was she really dead?

I snorted in disbelief. Apparently, girls lacked the tenacity of dogs. They should watch and learn from a dog's relentless will to live. At least then they wouldn't die like this, in such an uninteresting way.

    For now, I'd have to remove all traces of myself from the girl. After searching Yellow Scarf's body, I finally managed to find her phone inside her jacket pocket. The device broke easily in half when I threw it on the ground. I picked up the pieces and placed them in my trouser pocket, and trampling heavily on the scarf, which was sprawling limply on the ground like a boa constrictor, I climbed onto the seat of my bike. Before pedaling away, I took one last good look at the girl's face. Now that her skin had grown pale, she looked even more like the actress. Rest in peace…what was her name again? Anyway, Yellow Scarf.

    Then I pedaled off at great speed. My heart felt lighter. A whistle even escaped my lips. As I left the parking lot and headed for home, I didn't forget to toss the phone into the waste heap of the recycling center.

    Like that, Yellow Scarf's death and I became completely unrelated.

When I got home, I was overcome by fatigue.

    To stay awake I took a shower and then worked on my math problems in a more relaxed state of mind. It wasn't long before my tutor arrived, earlier than usual. She watched me work as she leaned against the door, and out of politeness I *pretended not to notice her there. I couldn't be bothered to reveal that I knew, anyway. After a while, I asked her what she was doing, and she quickly sat down, flustered. I could tell that she was unusually tense. Had she seen what had taken place in the parking lot?*

But the likelihood of that was very low. She didn't usually walk in that direction. The probability that the tutor had passed that site at that hour was therefore lower than the probability of snow in April.

I snuck a glance at her. She seemed completely lost in thought. Just then she raised her head, so I quickly pretended to be working. A short while later she spoke, sounding serious:

"Apparently someone saw your brother kill a dog. Did you know about that?"

For a moment I doubted my ears.

How does she know about that incident that happened last year?

I was stunned and excited.

I couldn't believe there was someone else who thought my brother had done it. Had she been caught up in the throng that had looked on as Umma and that woman argued? It wouldn't be so weird for her to believe that, if this was the case. Whatever — I couldn't believe that someone like her was here, right now, teaching me! This was the most interesting thing that had happened since the start of the new year.

Right then, my intuition was telling me that this was the perfect moment to tell her about my great artistic endeavors.

"Have you never wanted to kill anyone, miss?"

Her eyes widened, as if in surprise. I could barely contain the laughter that threatened to burst out of me.

"Well, if I said no, that would be a lie."

I'd won the lottery.

But of course — my intuition had hit the mark. If anyone could understand me, it would be this woman. I admitted to her that all of it — from the incident last year to the recent dog killings in the neighborhood — had been my handiwork. Now she'll admire me, won't she?

My heart racing with excitement, I awaited her response. But I was disappointed when she rebuked me, asking why I'd done those things when the animals had done nothing wrong. Done nothing wrong? They hadn't done anything wrong?

I couldn't hide my disappointment. In the end, she was like all the rest of those idiots. Feeling sorry for her, I explained what they were guilty of. But it still seemed like she couldn't understand. In fact, she asked me something pathetic and infinitely embarrassing: You didn't feel anything like a guilty conscience? I felt sad. I'd had faith in her intelligence.

"Why are you being so serious when it's not even a big deal? It's no fun."

I wanted to end this irritating conversation quickly.

Looking depressed, the tutor suddenly asked if she could

use the bathroom. I told her she could. I thought it might also help my mental health if she went away.

"I'll be back soon, so work on those problem sheets."

Then she left the room, taking her bag with her. Addressing the back of her head, I told her to take her time. She'd left with her bag, so it was clearly that time of the month. Was it because of this that she'd been so prickly earlier? This is why women are so difficult. Just then, out of the blue, I heard a clinking sound coming from the kitchen.

"Is that you, miss?" I asked loudly.

"Y-yes."

"What are you doing there?"

"I was just getting some water."

Why was she opening the fridge in someone else's home without permission? It rankled me. Soon she entered the room, and she was holding something that hadn't been in her hands when she'd left. Looking closely, I realized it was cheesecake, a personal favorite of mine.

"This is actually going to be our last class together. Something's come up, you see. I'm sorry I couldn't tell you in advance. Oh, and today's your birthday, isn't it? This is my birthday gift. It's been fun."

I hadn't been expecting this speech. I was a little startled by the sudden announcement, but I didn't feel all that sorry about it. If it hadn't been for that conversation today, it would be a different story, of course. Goodbye, miss. I don't *need you now. I'll find someone else who'll understand me. Someone less stupid than you.*

"I had fun, too, miss. I'll enjoy the cake."

The tutor seemed relieved. For a very brief second, I thought I saw her give a meaningful smile, but — was I mistaken?

Anyway, shall I get started on the work again? I think I saw one tied up in front of the bicycle shop on my way here earlier. Well, there's still plenty of time. I'll have a think while I eat this cake.

4.
YOU ARE A BAD MOTHER
[MIRA'S VISIT]

Hello, Yujae's mother.

Ah, now that Yujae isn't around, do I call you Yuchan's mother? But are you not feeling well? You've turned very pale. Are you not glad to see me? But I'm so happy to see you, after so long.

You must be wondering how I found my way to your home. May I elaborate once we're inside? I was visiting some other place before coming here, so my legs are aching.

This place looks smaller than your previous home. Is it about thirty pyeong? Still, this should be spacious enough for two people. Though uncomfortable, of course, since it's smaller than your old home. I'll have some black tea, please, not coffee.

Oh, I almost forgot. I didn't want to come empty-handed, so I bought some macarons from the department store on my way here. I'm not sure if they'll be to your taste, Ms. Moon. In any case, it must be so nice to live here, with a department store nearby and everything. I heard house prices in this area are quite expensive. Well, it's Gangnam, so of course it'd be expensive. I'm somewhat of a layman when it comes to real estate.

I assume you returned to Korea last week? Seeing as you haven't finished unpacking yet.

How was life in Australia? Yuchan wrote in an email that Melbourne was possibly the best city to live in the world. How did I end up exchanging emails with him? I'll explain that a little later. Anyway, I could see why he'd said that once I saw the photos he'd attached to his email. The place called the Arts Center Melbourne looked very similar to the Eiffel Tower in Paris. And you spent two years in a place like that—how wonderful it must have been! If I were you I wouldn't have wanted to return to Korea, probably.

But still, there's no place as comfortable as your own country. Australia's notorious for its White Australia policy, isn't it? You must have experienced it yourself while you were over there, Ms. Moon. Yuchan was bullied at school, wasn't he? You didn't know? He told me so himself. Countless times he'd be walking down the street and for no reason at all someone would try to pick a fight with him. More than once, he wanted to die, that's what he wrote in his letters. How he must have suffered, if he went so far as to bring it up with me when we didn't even know each other that well. And then he was telling me how he couldn't bring himself to talk to you about it. When I asked him why, what was it he said... I'm sorry. I'm just so tired right now, that must be why my brain isn't working very well.

But were you really not aware of these things?

But you told me yourself that there's not a single parent out there who doesn't know what's going on in their children's lives. I guess there are exceptions to that rule, then?

You must have so many things you want to ask me. Now I'll tell you my story in earnest.

What happened two years ago after December 16 — all of it.

Before that, may I use the restroom?

I've kept you waiting, haven't I?

As you already know, I'm not usually one to fumble for words, but this time I can't seem to figure out where or how to start. I'll try going back to my final tutorial with Yujae, first. That day, I took home what remained of the potassium cyanide, after placing it in the front pocket of my bag. You must have noticed because the whole thing would have disappeared. It wasn't intentional, at all. Yujae suddenly asked me in a loud voice what I was doing, and in a flutter, I made the mistake of putting it inside my bag, which I then forgot about. When I got home and opened my bag, there it was, the bottle of potassium cyanide.

I was extremely shocked. And also frightened. My mind began to race, thinking about how I should get rid of it. The idea of pouring it down the sink made me feel uneasy since, after all, that's where you wash the dishes. It was the same for the toilet. I didn't want to wash it down the drain, but I didn't feel like throwing the whole bottle in the bin, either. It would be a disaster if it broke while being discarded and a stray cat happened to lick at the liquid.

As I had no idea how to get rid of it, I simply returned it to the front pocket of my bag. I thought keeping it somewhere close at hand would be the safest option. Since at least I knew what it was.

Shall I take a guess at what you're thinking right now?

You probably want to rant, Why didn't you just throw it away! Your face has grown very red. Here, try some of these dark chocolate macarons. Dark chocolate will help soothe your agitation.

Oh, and I received the letter you sent me from Australia. Kim Minhyeok told you where I was staying, didn't he? I was annoyed at first that he'd done such a pointless thing, but once I read your letter I almost felt grateful to him.

You really came up with a plausible-sounding story. It very nearly fooled me.

You must have sent that letter to dupe me completely, but that was a mistake on your part. I wouldn't have been this angry, you see, if you hadn't sent that letter.

Maybe it's fate. If I'd thrown away the bottle, I'd have been in the dark forever. I wouldn't have had a reason to contact Yuchan or come looking for you like this.

Would that have been preferable? Would it have made everyone happy?

I think it would have only made you happy, Ms. Moon. Since no one else wanted that.

You get it now, don't you? How selfish your actions were? I'll admit it. Your scheme was a success.

I mean, it could have been a disaster. Without knowing the truth, I almost ended up being deceived by you.

Just as I expected, you didn't report me to the police. I knew I could count on you to have Yujae's death declared an accident. Not that you would do it on my account. It was something you had to do to protect your pride and dignity as well. You know better than anyone what kind of person you are, Ms. Moon. You're not exactly someone who's kind-natured enough to consider other people's circumstances, are you?

You didn't think you were, surely?

But you turned out to be a far more selfish and frightening person than I'd realized.

It's not that you didn't report it to the police. Whether for your sake or mine.

It's that nothing worth reporting had occurred in the first place.

Two years ago, as I wrote in my letter, I went down to Jeju Island four days after the incident. The boardinghouse I was staying at was a wonderful place located near the Hyeopjae beach resort, with rooms that offered a view of the sea. During the day I went walking by the shore, and at night I read books. Other than myself, there were three other people there—a woman in her mid-thirties, who had divorced her husband and decided on a whim to come down with her nine-year-old son, and an aspiring writer in his early forties.

In the beginning, no one spoke to the others. Everyone wanted peace and quiet. They'd come here for that. It was only after bumping into one another in the kitchen several times that we began to disclose, little by little, why we were there. I made up some lie, of course. I said I'd wanted some fresh air. Thankfully, everyone just took me at my word. I got the impression they were trying not to ask too many questions, out of consideration for me. I felt the same way. None of us thought it was considerate to be too interested in one another's lives.

The problem was the little boy. The son of the divorcée, I mean.

Since you've raised two sons, I'm sure you'll sympathize— with just how inquisitive and impolite boys are at that age.

One day, over coffee, the woman and I were discussing a TV morning drama. I was engrossed in the conversation, not realizing that her son was rooting around in my bag. I'd been careless, leaving a bag containing poison lying around. Even when the child shouted, "Wow, it's a drink!" I hadn't the slightest idea what kind of situation was unfurling. It was only after I heard the child's mother scold him, "I told you not to touch other people's bags without permission!" that I realized what was going on, but by then it was too late. The child was already swallowing the liquid.

Surely you can guess how shocked I was just then?

I thought I was going into cardiac arrest. I should have just thrown it away in the bin. Now, within the next three seconds, that child's heart will stop beating. He's going to die because of me. Me. How do I explain this to his mother? During that brief second as the child swallowed the liquid, all sorts of thoughts crossed my mind.

But what do you think happened to the child?

Yes, you're right. What you're thinking right now, Ms. Moon, is exactly what happened.

The boy was perfectly fine. Even though he'd drunk the whole bottle without leaving behind a single drop. Actually, he was upset that it wasn't a soda. If that was the case, how was the child able to live instead of dying? Was it a miracle of the human body? Have you ever heard of a case where someone survived after drinking potassium cyanide?

At once, all kinds of doubts descended on me.

Could it be that the liquid in the bottle hadn't contained any potassium cyanide in the first place? Then what was it exactly that I'd given to Yujae that day?

I grew dazed, as if my head had collided with a wall. What words can express the shock I'd felt just then?

I had to find out where things had started to go wrong.

The thing that made the least sense to me was your letter.

Because there, you'd clearly written that Yujae had died from ingesting potassium cyanide. There was no way a parent would be so mistaken about their offspring's death. No matter how many possible scenarios I conjured up, it just wouldn't add up.

I needed someone who'd be able to confirm the truth for me.

Someone who was close to you but held the middle ground.

Yes, that person was Yuchan.

I was able to get hold of his email address without much difficulty by contacting his former school. Immediately I sent him a long letter describing what I'd gone through. All I could do after that was to wait for his reply. A whole week went by, but he wasn't even checking his inbox. My nerves were so on edge, it was unbearable. The entire time I waited, I was unable to have a single decent night's sleep.

Then one day, it appeared he'd finally checked his email. But can you believe this time he didn't respond for an entire month? Again I was plagued by insomnia. And just when I was about to tell myself it was time to give up, his reply arrived. Do you want to know what it said? To my relief, the message said he would help me. It felt like I'd discovered an oasis in the middle of a desert.

As it turned out, Yuchan already knew that it was his brother who'd tried to kill him. It seemed to have shaken him very badly. Every day that he spent living with his brother felt like hell, he said. To be honest, after learning that kind of truth, who can remain unaffected? Especially if the person who tried to harm you is none other than your little brother.

Oh, and Yuchan also seemed to hold a great deal against you.

You don't look like you believe me. I was expecting that, so I've printed out some of the messages. Wait a minute, I definitely put them in here. Oh, here they are. He sent me several diary entries that he wrote two years ago. I guess he wanted to make his position very clear. Shall I read them aloud, if that's all right with you? That way it'll give you less of a shock than reading it yourself.

November 19

There are only three things that Umma wants from me: rank number one; Seoul National University; Korea's greatest mathematician.

When I was little, I thought I really was a genius.

"You're a genius, so it'll be like eating cold porridge for you." That was something Umma would say, habitually. And so I believed myself to be a genius, and I tried hard to make it look that way. I'd always get full marks in math. While other kids my age fretted over a single problem, I'd solve seven more. Of course, I did find the subject interesting. I could scarcely put into words the feeling I'd get whenever I came across a new mathematical formula. All the numbers I saw in day-to-day life were my toys: car license plates, bus numbers, telephone numbers, postal codes, street numbers, street signs, and more.

In my third year of middle school, I took part in the International Mathematical Olympiad. I was the only middle school student on the team.

But I ended up receiving an awful score in the competition. I simply couldn't keep up with kids from India, China, the USA, and Europe. I tasted a kind of defeat I'd never experienced until then. That was when I discovered I wasn't a genius.

After that, I sank into a deep rut. It reached a point where recovery looked impossible. I managed to get into a science high school with my basic mathematical ability, but my grades kept sliding. I'd show Umma forged report cards, and then every day I'd shrivel up inside with fear that she'd call the school to check.

The results of the practice exam came out today. They were below expectations, as I'd thought.

I resent it. If only Umma hadn't said stuff like that.

If she hadn't told me I was a genius, I wouldn't have felt this frustrated. If she hadn't been so fixated on me, I wouldn't have felt so much guilt.

It's suffocating. I don't have what it takes to be Korea's greatest mathematician. But Umma expects this of me. I don't have the confidence to tell her that her hopes are in vain.

I want to run away. I feel pathetic for not being able to do it.

I'm a coward. I'm an idiot and a fool.

November 20

I was listening to Seo Taiji's "Tank" to clear my mind a bit. His music refreshes me; it's like a weight is being lifted off my chest. As the song neared its end, my brother came into my room, his face pale with fright. What was the matter, I asked without interest, wanting to be alone, and he said he'd coughed up blood. For a moment a chill went down my spine like I'd been doused with cold water. We weren't very close, but I grew afraid at the thought that he might die. I did my best to appear unruffled, however. My brother was in shock, so at least I should try to act calm and collected.

First of all, I told him to go back and wait in his room, and then I called a friend whose older brother was a doctor *specializing in internal medicine. The friend said he'd ask his brother and call me back in a bit. I'll always be grateful to him. He rang me about ten minutes later. Going by a description alone, it was difficult to make an accurate diagnosis, his brother had said, but from what he could see from his overall condition, it didn't seem very serious. I was relieved. At last I could breathe properly. I wanted to tell Yujae at once that he could put his mind at ease.*

As I made my way to his room, I was struck by a sudden thought. Apparently, before people die, they normally recall the people they've hurt over the years. No doubt my brother would have done the same. He would have called to mind the animals that suffered because of him. And then he'd have done some soul-searching. If he hadn't, this was the time to do it, I thought. It would be for his own good, after all.

I know what Yujae's been up to, late at night. Not that I'd known from the start. I found out only recently, to be honest. Last Sunday, I was having trouble falling asleep, so I'd gone to the convenience store at around 2 a.m. to get something to drink when by chance I discovered a gang of middle school students hanging around in the empty lot. There were about five or six of them. At that hour, there are only so many things adolescent boys can get up to: smoking, or harassing others.

It was just as I was hurrying past, not wanting to get drawn into anything, that I noticed. A boy resembling Yujae seemed to be mingling with the group. Surely not, I thought, staring with narrowed eyes. I hadn't been wrong. My brother was kicking at something. I couldn't see what it was, obscured as it was by their bodies. I shuffled several steps to one side. It turned out to be a small puppy. The boys snickered every time my brother kicked the puppy like a football.

Even as I looked on with my eyes, I couldn't believe what I was seeing. I deliberately made the noise of footsteps. As the boys glanced briefly in my direction, the puppy took that moment to make its escape, and with a disgruntled "For fuck's sake," they scattered. Perhaps because it was so dark, my brother didn't seem to recognize me.

When had he started doing something like that?

I'd known since we were little that he was a bit different, but I didn't know it was like this. Does Umma know? If she finds out, she'll be appalled. It might be better to keep this from her.

I told Yujae what I'd seen. When I told him that he ought to feel remorseful about the animal he'd tormented and its owner, and he should refrain from doing it again, he fixed me with an unreadable expression. I thought he seemed discomfited by the fact that his clandestine activities had been exposed. For a moment he appeared lost in thought, but then he replied, saying he'd do as I asked.

I felt ill at ease. In a way, my brother, too, was a victim.

He'd never received our mother's attention, which was why he kept going astray.

I used to feel sorry that I had her attention all to myself. So I'd racked my brain to see if there was anything I could do for him, but I hadn't been able to find a solution. We'd already grown too far apart.

It had been a long while since both my brother and I remembered how to approach each other.

November 27

I never really could socialize with girls.

It'd been like that since elementary school. All around me, there were always other boys, hordes of them. It wasn't that I was shy or had no interest. I'm not all that introverted. That's not to say I don't feel anything toward the opposite sex. The reason was plain and simple. Umma didn't like it when I talked to girls.

She always kept an eye on me. She inspected my phone regularly, and if she found a girl's name she'd ask me who she was, how I knew her, whether she was a good student, and so on, as if she was conducting an interrogation, and then she'd delete the number. Since she kept probing whether the girl was a good student, I thought it would be okay if the girl in question was a good student. But that wasn't the case. Umma would talk as though it was some kind of calamity if I was with a girl, whoever she was.

"What are you going to do if you fail the Suneung exam as a result? It's more than enough to date people after you get into university."

Then she'd always try to comfort me with these words:

"It's all for your own good, Yuchan. Though you're too young to know that."

But there's one thing my grown-up mother doesn't know.

The more people forbid you to do something, the more you want to do it — that's natural human psychology. Just as how, in the Bible, Adam and Eve fell for the snake's ploy and ended up eating the apple.

Several days ago, a snake appeared, one that was going to awaken my instincts, which until now had been inhibited by the prohibition.

She was a small and cute-looking girl. Anyone could have believed she was the younger sister of the actress Song Hye-kyo.

Judging by her uniform, she seemed to be in middle school. She came all the way to my school to look for me, and after wordlessly handing me a letter, she skipped away and disappeared. It turned out to be a love letter. Beside me, my classmates were saying how envious they were, elbowing me in the ribs. Honestly, at first I was dumbfounded. Nothing like this had ever happened to me before, so I didn't know how I was supposed to respond. It said in the letter that she'd first seen me on the bus. The next day, she came looking for me again and handed me a letter. And again the next day, and the day after that...

She said her name was Yi Songhui.

Songhui. It was a name as pretty as her face.

December 1

Today she asked me if she could call me Yuchan oppa. My heart trembled in spite of myself. Yuchan oppa. And then, before I could even reply, she kissed me on the lips and ran away. It was my first-ever kiss. I don't remember what face I was making right then. I probably looked very stupid.

Oh, even now my heart feels like it might explode.

I'd better write her a reply today, too.

December 7

It's been exactly a week since I started exchanging messages with her without Umma's knowledge.

But my mother seems to have got wind of something. It'll get risky starting tomorrow, so I'd better hold back on the letter writing. I'll save her number on my phone under a boy's name. That way Umma won't suspect anything.

December 11

We took advantage of our lunch and dinner breaks to meet in front of the school building. When I'm with her, I want to live. I want to see her face and hear her voice every day. It's fascinating. Songhui possesses things that I don't have. She smiles often, she's lively, she never loses her nerve, and she's assertive. Most of all, I like her sense of freedom. She's not like the coward I am, locked inside a birdcage.

Today, she asked if we could go on a date. Tomorrow, at 8 p.m. The spot was in front of the pedestrian overpass, near C Elementary School. I couldn't reply to her right away. Why in front of the overpass, of all places, when there were so many other spots. Songhui said she wanted to go to that café on the other side of the road with me. Though I didn't feel like it, I agreed so as not to disappoint her.

Will I be able to cross the overpass? I'm already worried.

March 7 (*This is from the diary he kept after recovering from his coma.*)

I'm confused. I'm so confused I think I'm going crazy.

    I can't forget the feel of her hands pushing against my back that day. Like a leech, the sensation is still stuck to my back and won't come off.

Why? What had I done to her that was so wrong she'd want to kill me?

I want to know. No, I have to know. I have a right to know. I tried calling her phone, but it was already an unregistered number. I'd expected that. She must have changed her number after doing this to me.

I'd better pay a visit to her school tomorrow.

March 8

I waited outside the gates of her school, but in the end she didn't make an appearance. Has she quit school as well?

March 9

Today I grabbed every student leaving by the school gates to ask what year they were in. And I asked every student who said they were in their second year if they knew Yi Songhui. No one said they knew who she was. I was desperate. Millions of thoughts began to race through my mind. Was she not enrolled at this school? Had she borrowed her sister's uniform, or a friend's? Was her name even Yi Songhui? She might not be in middle school. High school, then? Surely not elementary school? Was it true she'd seen me on the bus? Why had she come looking for me? Had it all been an act?

Just then, someone tapped me on the shoulder. Turning

around, I found myself facing a chubby-cheeked girl wearing a pair of horn-rimmed glasses. "Are you looking for Songhui, by any chance?" she asked, sounding like she had a cold. When I nodded, her expression swiftly turned despondent. She knows something, my intuition told me. My heart began to race. A moment later, she told me, crying…

My hands are shaking so hard that I don't think I can write this bit.

March 10

I couldn't fall asleep last night.

Songhui has been murdered.

Based on what her friend told me yesterday, she'd been a victim of random murder, a case of "don't ask why" killing.

I knew the site where her body had been discovered. The parking lot beside the church.

When I learned the date of her death, I was so shocked that my hands and feet became paralyzed. She'd died barely a week after I'd fallen into a coma. There was something too disturbing about it to call it a coincidence.

Who had murdered Songhui? Had it really been a "don't ask why" murder? Why had Songhui tried to kill me?

Were the two incidents somehow related?

Now that I think about it, she'd said something unexpected to me at the top of the overpass: Don't trust your brother too much. How had Songhui known my brother? What was their relationship? Could he be somehow connected to the two incidents? Had he used her to try to kill me, and then killed her because she was no longer useful? But what for, exactly?

I don't get it. I don't understand anything.

But if my guesses are correct, how am I supposed to live now? Will I be able to pretend I don't know anything, and treat my brother the same way as before?

I'm not sure I can do it. I'm not sure I'll be able to live and breathe in the same space as someone who tried to kill me.

I feel anxious. Anxious and scared. It's like I'm trapped in a dark cave by myself.

Does Umma know it was my brother who did it? Or doesn't she?

I don't know. I can't trust anyone now. Not my mother, nor my brother.

I'm scared of him.

He'll try to kill me again someday. There's no doubt about it. Since Songhui suffered the same fate in the end.

The above are the diary entries Yuchan sent me.

Are you crying? Then, wipe with a tissue. We're not at the part yet where you should be crying. After all, the really important part begins now.

If I were to summarize your scheme, it probably went something like this:

Deliberately, you show the tutor the fake potassium cyanide you've prepared in advance. You let her know via text message that the real object of her resentment has to be Yujae. The reason you go to that effort is because it'll make it easier later to deceive the tutor by bringing up your own legitimate motive for murder. Having recalled the potassium cyanide, the tutor uses it in her revenge play. Then she quits her job in the belief that she has taken revenge on Yujae. To secure the deception, you send her a letter. By admitting that it was you who killed Yujae, you pretend to console her and persuade her to forget the whole affair. Here you emphasize once again that Yujae is dead. But in reality, the oblivious boy is very much alive and well. Next, you take your two sons with you as you escape to Australia. Two years later, you return to Korea without the tutor's knowledge. Yujae lives his life in the open as a high school student.

How's that, for a guess?

Were you thinking of writing the ending to this entire story all by yourself? It would have been easy to fool me since potassium cyanide is colorless, anyway, when it's dissolved in water. All this time I'd been running around in the palm of your hand.

There are some things I still don't understand.

What made you stage this play?

You knew it was Yujae who'd tried to harm Yuchan, but why didn't you discipline him in any way? Why did you go around looking for the suspect with such vehemence?

It's the same with the dog-killing incidents.

When I made inquiries at the local police station, they told me they'd had no reported incidents of teenagers committing animal abuse in the last three years. Were you unable to report them out of fear that your son might get punished, too? You must have suddenly developed a fondness for your son that wasn't there before. And all the while, you lied to me shamelessly.

How many more people must suffer harm because of your selfishness, Ms. Moon? Do you intend to take measures once a second Songhui shows up? How many more animals must die in agony? Did you think it wouldn't matter what happened to anyone else as long as your children were safe? Did you never bother to think about it from Yuchan's perspective even as he shook in fear, living with his brother?

You told me yet another lie earlier. You knew that Yuchan was being bullied at school. Wasn't that the reason you decided to come back to Korea?

But once you decided to return, my existence here would have weighed on your mind. You couldn't let it be known that Yujae was still alive, after all. That's probably why you moved here, deliberately. Why wouldn't you be living in your old home, if not for that? There are tenants renting that place right now, aren't there? I already went to check. You're their landlord, as it turns out.

Just to make things clear, I was the one who made you return to Korea.

I asked Yuchan to act like he was being bullied. I told him to make it as obvious to you as possible that he was struggling to adjust to life in Australia. So that, you see, there would be no other option but to return to Korea. As I'd predicted, if it had anything to do with your children, it made you tremble like a leaf. At this sensitive moment in time, with Yuchan's future hanging in the balance, you would have been even more concerned. It was about two years later that a message finally arrived from Yuchan. It said that he'd be returning to Korea within the month.

You probably won't know how ecstatic I was to hear this news.

Again, it was Yuchan who told me the address of this place. And then once he was back in the country, he followed suit with the name of Yujae's school and his phone number.

I told you earlier that I visited someplace before I came here.

Yes, that's right.

I was actually on my way back from meeting him. He's attending a great school. His uniform looks very fine.

I sent him a message saying I was standing in front of his school, wouldn't he like to meet up for a brief chat? He replied that it was in the middle of a class right now, so he'd come out to meet me during the break. And true to his word, I could see a male student strolling out from the school gates twenty minutes later. He seemed remarkably glad to see me, perhaps because of how long it'd been since we last saw each other. He looked very well. He'd grown even more handsome. He must be popular with the girls. He'd started to look quite grown-up now.

We chatted for a few minutes. He'd read a lot of books in the meantime. Wouldn't it have been wonderful if he'd just put that exceptional head of his to more worthwhile pursuits? Asking him if he wasn't feeling cold, I handed him a thermos flask I'd prepared in advance. I'd noticed in passing long ago that the boy really liked peanut butter cookies. So I'd prepared peanut butter-flavored coffee specially for him. As I'd hoped, he was thrilled. He didn't seem to suspect anything in the slightest. Saying he wanted to save it for later so he could drink it during the evening study period, he asked if he could take the flask with him, and I said yes, of course. It didn't worry me at all. As you know, the boy isn't exactly the kindhearted type who'd share something tasty with his friends.

It won't be long now before a phone call arrives from his school.

Unlike you, I didn't play any tricks. A close friend of mine happens to work as a chemistry teacher at a middle school, so I was able to obtain the potassium cyanide without much difficulty.

Do you have a resentful and aggrieved expression?

Or is it that, at long last, you're feeling pity for Yujae?

When you told me that there's nothing you can't do for your son, you must have been referring to Yujae. He's still your son, I see, even if he's human trash. You strike me as a far more pitiful figure, Ms. Moon.

In your letter to me, you described yourself as a bad mother to your firstborn son, didn't you?

You're wrong.

To make a slight correction, I'd say you were a bad mother to both of your sons.

You discriminated between them to an excessive degree, and you watched in silence even as your offspring went off in the wrong direction. That would be the difference between you and your husband. If he were still alive, would he have pretended not to know about Yujae's misdeeds, and simply let him be? Your inaction and selfishness ended up plunging both children into misery.

There's no need to feel aggrieved.

As you wrote in your letter, they may only be teenagers, but if they've committed a crime, they should be punished for it. You also said that parents are to blame for 90 percent of the child's wrongdoing. Wouldn't this mean that you ought to be punished, too, Ms. Moon?

And now the phone must be ringing, right? Go on, do pick it up. Though it's already too late, even if you do.

I'm thinking of reporting the other five boys to the police tomorrow morning. I only know the name of one of them, of course, but once I report the student named Oh Dong-gyu, I'm sure I can leave the rest to him. There's nothing as flimsy as the camaraderie of teenage boys, you see.

It's not like I haven't considered things from Yujae's perspective, of course. I did wonder if I wasn't being too calm and dispassionate. For all that, he's only just a high school student.

He couldn't have expected this, either.

That his petty lie would become a lethal poisoned needle that would snatch away people's lives. And more than that, he could never have imagined that the same needle would veer around and hurtle toward himself.

I understand. It's true, then, that I do feel a tiny bit apologetic toward him. I'm only human, so surely it's to be expected that I'd feel that much sympathy.

But isn't it precisely our lives whose futures we can't ever peer into, even by an inch?

How would I have known that I'd lose my mother and brother in the space of a morning? Like how you've just lost a son.

So, the question of whether you could have predicted it or not should be considered a separate problem from the issue of forgiveness. You may not have known it would lead to tragedy, but the act of lying was wrong from the start. No matter how petty the lie might have been.

Well, it may be entirely meaningless to think such thoughts now. We've come too far already. As Yuchan wrote in his diary.

Is that the time already?

I should go before it gets too late. Earlier, on my way here, it looked pretty cloudy, like it might rain. Ah, I wouldn't want to bump into each other in the future, even on the street. Won't that be better for the both of us?

Then goodbye.

AUTHOR'S NOTE

I've always wanted to write things that can make contact with me from up close.

And before long, I find myself—along with the question How might I express in words the priceless value of a life?—feeling like something unknowable, like a very dark space.

Life is a riddle that can never be solved, and it may be in order to soothe this riddle, and stroke it gently, that I continue to write fiction.

I'm pleased and delighted to be able to meet you through my debut novel, *Petty Lies*.

After you close the book, I hope it'll linger richly in your mind, like the glow of the sun against the horizon.

I add these words that will never get tired, even if they're repeated hundreds of times:

This book is for my beloved family.

Autumn 2025

ABOUT THE AUTHOR

Sulmi Bak, born in 1984, majored in journalism and chose the path of a novelist while preparing for the entrance exam of Korea's top game company. *Petty Lies* is her debut novel, followed by two other stand-alone novels, *The Silence of the Swan* and *Dalwhinnie Hotel*.